SULLY

DANI RENÉ

Dear Reader,

There are parts of this story that have been extremely difficult to write. When I first sat down with Clover's journey, I knew it wasn't going to be easy to write certain scenes, and I was right.

But it had to be done.

I hope that anyone who is in a similar situation can find the strength to get out. And those who have escaped, I hope you find the peace and solace you deserve. Sending love...

Mad love,

Dani, xo

ROYAL BASTARDS MC
BELFAST, NORTHERN IRELAND

WARNING

Sully is a dark grey romance that contains scenes of domestic abuse that can be a trigger to certain readers. Please be careful before reading further.

ROYAL BASTARDS CODE

PROTECT: The club and your brothers come before anything else, and must be protected at all costs. CLUB is FAMILY.

RESPECT: Earn it & Give it. Respect club law. Respect the patch. Respect your brothers. Disrespect a member and there will be hell to pay.

HONOR: Being patched in is an honor, not a right. Your colors are sacred, not to be left alone, and NEVER let them touch the ground.

OL' LADIES: Never disrespect a member's or brother's Ol'Lady. PERIOD.

CHURCH is MANDATORY.

LOYALTY: Takes precedence over all, including well-being.

HONESTY: Never LIE, CHEAT, or STEAL from another member or the club.

TERRITORY: You are to respect your brother's property and follow their Chapter's club rules.

TRUST: Years to earn it...seconds to lose it.

NEVER RIDE OFF: Brothers do not abandon their family.

PLAYLIST

The Wrong One - One Less Reason

Drink my Stupid Away - Royal Bliss

A Day to be Alone - One Less Reason

Skin Deep - Memory of a Melody

Somewhere I Belong - Angels Fall

All Beauty Fades - One Less Reason

Find the full playlist on Spotify

In distant days
Their fate entwined
Unaware of secrets
That lay confined

Passions bloomed
As souls aligned
Truth's cruel arrival
Would disrupt their time

These unveiling ties
Would test the hearts
Pulling her away
Ripping them apart

Months would pass
His search led him back
He belonged with her
Nothing could change that

Found
_hydrus

More from Hydrus at

www.hydruspoetry.com

DEDICATION

To the women who escaped, survived, and thrived.
To those still in the dark, you are strong and
you can get out.

PROLOGUE

I grin down at the motherfecker who's bearin' down on the metal between his yellowed teeth. Both his eyes are swelling with purple bruises that will soon turn blue. He's tryin'ta speak, but there's nothin' he can say that will change the fact he's been leakin' information about our shipments to the mob.

It's not the first time Monster has allowed one of us ta take the lead, and I'm thankful I'm able to take this one. The metal knuckle-dusters I wrap my fingers around glint in the sunlight streamin' through the window.

"The last time ye decide to feck with the Royal Bastards will be today. We don't take kindly ta rats, and when ye run off and tell yer friends about our shipments, we need ta send a message," I tell him, keepin' my voice controlled, yet drippin' pure venom.

"Mmh uh mm," he bites out through the metal, and I smile.

Rearing back, I bring my fist down on his jaw, listening to the crack that follows, and I can't help but feel satisfied. I won't kill him, not this time. We want him to go back ta them and show them just how fecking ruthless we are.

"I'm the feckin' cleaner, and I'll gladly clean yer blood off this floor," I tell him. "I'll make sure ye remember me—remember the Royal feckin' Bastards." Stepping back, I motion for the two prospects ta take the arsehole's shirt off.

"Hey," Rebel calls from behind me as he enters the warehouse.

This place is a shitehole, but Monster likes it because it's outside the city, and nobody comes here.

I turn to Rebel and notice he has Hades with him as well. "What's goin' on?" I ask.

"Monster wants us in church in an hour," Rebel tells

me.

I glance at the man we caught, and I shake my head before I release the metal from my knuckles and lean in to look directly into his eyes. The terror that flits in them makes me happy. I love watchin' someone cower in fear. And right now, I grip the arsehole's throat and squeeze.

"Ye tell all yer wee friends they'll pay a hefty price if they attempt to trade in our territory. Ye'll also inform them every feckin' piece of information you spewed to them is false. Make them believe it. Do you understand me?"

He nods quickly, his head movin' so fast it's a blur for a second or two. Tears fill his eyes as he watches me. My fingers tighten, a warnin', and then I release him.

"Get this arsehole out of here," I order before I head over ta Rebel and Hades. The two prospects shove the black bag over his head and drag him from the chair. Once they're out of earshot, I ask my two brothers. "So, church?"

Hades is the one who answers, "Tye has some information on Bragan."

"I can't wait till we get that fecker and make him pay," I tell them as we make our way out to the bikes. Turnin' my key, I rev the engine, givin' Rebel and Hades a hint that I want a race.

The moment I pull away, they're close behind. It doesn't take us long ta reach the clubhouse. The adrenaline from the session at the warehouse is still fresh in my mind, but as I walk in, I can't stop the smile that curls my lips.

There, waitin' on me, is my girl.

My Lucky Clover.

CHAPTER 1

The Past
Twenty-Five Years Old

Death—the visitor that most of us try to escape. Nobody gets to do that, though, because it's the one thing in life that's a promise.

For some, the Reaper visits far too early. He comes knockin' when they least expect it, and then they have no choice but to walk with him into the afterlife.

That's when it hurts the most. The unexpected.

When it happens, it's an agony that nobody can describe, but also one that no person can run from. I don't believe in heaven or hell, even though I grew up havin'ta go ta church every feckin' Sunday, but somethin' about it never sat quite right with me. *How can one entity judge millions?* I'm not a believer, and even though I see miracles happen all around me every day, I also see the ugliness in the world.

As the plane comes in to land on the smooth tarmac, the wheels touch down with a thump and I take in the airport building. I'm finally in the US for the first time in a long while. I've flown across the pond before, but never on club business.

Monster, the President of the Royal Bastards MC in Belfast and one of my oldest friends, agreed I could fly over and represent the club. Which brings me here, to Washington State where The Kovenant MC is based. This part of the country is far more breathtakin' than anywhere else in the States. At least, that's what I think. White Pass is one place I've visited that felt like home. It's been a long time since I've been here, but now I'm back, I can't deny I've missed it.

It's a part of the world that's so vastly different to home, ta Belfast. It feels as if I'm in a completely foreign world. The men of the Kovenant have been friends of mine for a long while, and when I first came to America years ago, I befriended the man who's now the President of the club.

When I pull up to the clubhouse, I find a couple of the prospects at the gate. Both look like they're still fairly wet behind the ears, so ta speak, and I want ta chuckle at the way they look at me—fear and intrigue dancin' in their stares.

"I'm here ta see Sean," I say to them. "Ye can tell him Sully is here from Belfast." I don't kill the engine, so between that and the engines of the bikes rumblin' from the other side of the gate, I have to repeat myself before one of them nods quickly and rushes off ta make the call.

It doesn't take long until I'm slowly inchin' up the long driveway that leads to the main house. Since it's built between two enormous mountains, the views are breathtakin'.

The moment I turn off the bike, I take in the sights. There are still snow capped tips that are visible from down below. Nestled between the peaks, is the feckin' enormous mansion that Sean had built for the brothers. He reminds me so much of Monster. He's always treated the club members as his family. His wife passed away a couple of years ago from cancer, and I know he still misses her. Knowin' he's got the support of his brothers is a good thing. When you lose someone, it's never easy, but if you do it on your own, it can break you down slowly, day by day.

"Sully!" His booming tone comes from the doorway, and I swing my leg over the bike before makin' my way to one of my oldest friends. At forty-eight, he's aged since I last saw him—he has more salt than pepper in his hair, and the wrinkles are startin' to deepen on his face.

"Good ta see ye again, Sean," I tell him as we pull each other into a one-armed hug. Steppin' back, I gesture with my head. "This is a feckin' monster of a set up ye got here."

"It's been a long time coming. When we finally finished the building, I wanted to take a fucking holiday. But you know how life goes. Can't be walking away when there's shit to do."

I chuckle and nod. "Aye, yer tellin' me. There's a never-endin' list of jobs. Even when I'm not around, they're tellin' me what needs to be done next."

"Come," he says, before he turns and heads inside.

I follow behind, and I know that even though I'm not a part of the Kovenant, I'm a welcome guest.

Inside, I note how well kept the interior is. Most people don't imagine a place like this when you mention an MC clubhouse ta them. I've seen judgement on faces of strangers when they realise the leather cut I wear represents a gang of men who would do anything fer each other. It's happened ever since I joined the Royal Bastards. And I've no doubt the men of the Kovenant have been through the same.

"Nice," I say when we reach Sean's office.

He offers me a grin before he rounds a desk that sits at the far end of the room.

"It's my pride and joy," he tells me. "Well, one of them. The other is my daughter. After losing her mother, I've only got her to look after, and she's precious to me."

"Family is important," I respond easily as I settle into one of the brown armchairs that face the desk. "My ma was the only person I ever had ta worry about when I was young. I haven't seen her in so long, I wonder what's she's doin' now. Since joining Monster and the rest of the brothers, I realise I'm not entirely alone. I do have a family now."

Sean nods in understanding and says, "You'll always have one here too. You know that."

"Aye." I nod because it's true.

Sean settles into his chair and shuffles some pages

on the desk before he picks one up and hands it to me. When I scan the details, I realise why he needed me here. This has to do with the Irish mob.

"These men want to encroach on land they have no right to. The territories here are mine, and I don't share well."

He isn't smilin' anymore, and neither am I, because I know all about the feckers who Sean wants found. I'm the Cleaner of my club, but I know someone who can help with trackin' down anyone and everyone. Sean is lacking the one thing the Bastards have, and that's a tech guy.

"I can get Tye on this today," I tell Sean. "I don't think there's anythin', or anyone, he can't find. We've had some difficult jobs in the past few years, but the feckin' mob are snakes."

Sean chuckles as he leans back in his chair. "I've no doubt they're slithering around, waiting to attack. I want every one of them found."

He shakes his head, and I know it can't be easy fer him to even consider. I don't know if his wee girl misses her ma, but fer Sean, her passin' is still fresh in his mind. The pain of losin' someone ye love, someone who's been there with ye through difficulties, can't be easy. And then, there's the knowin' that you couldn't do anythin' ta stop the shite.

"We'll do this," I tell him. It's the most honesty I can offer right now.

"I'll have Ahren show you to your room," he tells me. I know the name. It's one of the newer prospects he was tellin' me about. "We're having a get together later in the bar. Just come down and join us. And tomorrow, we'll talk more."

It's gettin' late, and I'm probably goin'ta pass out fer a wee while, so I can stay focused tomorrow.

"Aye, I'll be there."

I follow Ahren out into the main area of the house. It's gettin' busier now with more of the brothers millin' around, and when I reach the top of the stairs, I find a hint of sweetness in the air. Ahren turns to the left, but my head whips to the right, and there, disappearin' into a bedroom is a wee dark-haired thing who captures my attention immediately. She doesn't see me, but the moment she shuts herself inside, I wonder just who she is.

"This is yours," Ahren tells me as we come to a stop outside the bedroom.

"I appreciate that, thanks." We shake hands, and I take in the younger lad. "How long have ye been with the club?"

"Only about a year now," he says, but the way he squares his shoulders, I can tell he's proud of bein' a member. "It's something I didn't think I'd want, but after I left my brother back in the small town he now calls home, I needed somewhere to belong."

I nod in understandin'. "Aye, I get that," I tell him. "I felt the same before I joined the Bastards. I think the need fer human connection is an instinct we all have."

"It's only ever been me and my brother, but when I found myself here, I realised I could have more of a family unit. Don't get me wrong, I love my brother, but I just wanted more."

"No bother, I understand ye," I tell him because I do.

Even though my mother is still in Ireland, I haven't seen her since since I was a teen. The club is the only place I can turn ta when I need support.

"I'll leave you to it," he says then. "Tonight will be a great party."

We say our goodbyes, and before I step into the bedroom I've been given, I can't help but allow my eyes to flick towards the door where the wee thing disappeared into. I'm not sure if she's a club whore, or if she's family, but one thing is fer sure, I want ta see her again.

In the room, I settle in at the desk which overlooks the back garden and pull out my phone. I need to get Tye workin' on the request from Sean, and hopefully, we can get him some closure. It's difficult to live with somethin' hangin' over ye head all the time.

When I scan my messages, I find one from the bastard who I asked fer help from, years ago—Ronan McCallum. He offered his hand, but then, the moment I took it, he dragged me into shite I never wanted to be a part of, and he knew it.

My past mistakes are filled with regret, but I won't ever regret what I did that day. I can't bring myself to think about it, so I force the memory from my mind. Once I have the message out to Tye, I delete the rest I've received. There isn't anythin' I can do from here, but the moment I'm back in Belfast, I'll be sortin' out the blackmailin' arsehole.

I need somethin' ta distract me, so I stand and head over ta the balcony. I shove open the doors and step out into the fresh air. The need for some nicotine runs through me.

Flickin' open the packet, I pull a cigarette out and press it between my lips. The moment the flame dances in front of my face, I inhale a deep lungful of much needed smoke, and that's when I see her. A tall, leggy brunette who's racin' down the garden towards the wall that surrounds the compound.

She can't climb it, so I'm intrigued as to what the feck she's doin'. Her tanned skin looks to be smooth and blemish free. Her Converse covered feet carry her out ta the perimeter, and that's when I see another girl, this one blonde, rushin' towards her. They're laughin' and gigglin' as they make their way back ta the house. They don't see me, but I certainly see them. Both are pretty, but it's the brunette who's captured my attention.

They're still laughin' as they settle on the lounge chairs. I can't deny myself the stunnin' view, and I stay outside far longer than I wanted. As the sun sets and they move to come inside, I do the same.

I should freshen up. The party is goin'ta be in full swing when I head downstairs, which is fine by me, as long as I get another glimpse of the pretty brunette. I couldn't tell her age from where I was standin', but I have a feelin' she'd be eighteen at least. That's my feckin' hope, because I want to cup her face in my hands and feel her lips on mine.

I haven't been with a woman in a fair while now, so a much needed night of fuckin' will be good. And right now, the only thing on my mind is the wee lass.

CHAPTER 2

The Past

Fifteen Years Old

Death—the visitor that most of us try to hide from, to run from.

Nobody *wants* to die, but there's no running from what's inevitable.

It's something that will touch each of us at some point in our lives. There are things in this world we can never escape, and the inevitable happens. And when it does, we either go to heaven or hell, depending on how we treated others in our lifetime and how we lived our lives. There are rules, commandments, we have to follow.

When I was a little girl, my father sat me down to tell me about my mama. At least, he tried to. I could tell he was hurting as much as I was. Possibly more. He'd lost a lifetime partner, and I'd lost my mother. Mama died from cancer, so I never had a chance to grow up with her around.

Dad had to ease my worries because I kept asking why she had to go away. I'd go to school and watch as the other kids' mothers dropped them off. Their mamas' would give them hugs and kisses, and I wanted that too.

Dad told me she was a woman that came with a force behind her. She was a storm raging through life, and he was the only one to tame her. For a time.

Over the years, he told me how much I reminded him of her. Now I'm a teenager, it's as if she's a living, breathing entity inside me. It's the only place I feel her. I've seen movies where people say they've lost loved ones and they don't feel them anymore. I guess I'm lucky. She's still here, looking out for me through my eyes.

Deep inside, I know she was strong. But even after all the stories my father told me about her, I've realized I'll only ever have *his version* of their life together.

I've pieced together the roller coaster my mama was on while being married to the man who raised me. It wasn't easy for her. Life never is. The photos we have at home show her as a happy, smiling woman. She doted on Dad, and it's obvious just how much she loved him in the way she looks at him in the pictures. Each one shows just how her gaze tracks his. They were the perfect couple until cancer stole her from him. There was unconditional love there. Pure love.

There wasn't anything tainting her view of him. Even though Dad has always been a part of the motorcycle club, he was good to her. He loved her more than he loved his own life. And now, I'm the only part of her that's left. And I know it hurts him that she's not here to see me grow up.

The men in my family come from a long line of heroes, confronting death, and forcing it to its knees. Once day, when I come face to face with death, dad taught me to look it right in the eye and not flinch. If it comes calling, I've always figured I'd be strong—that I'd be just like him. And I want that. There's no way

I'm going to be a weak person, not even in the face of danger.

Dad has made sure I've grown up with a hardened shell. I don't trust anyone who isn't part of the family, the club. The men who would do anything for my father are the same men who would do anything for me. And since I was a little girl, I've believed no one else matters. I've lived by the law of the club.

But as I wait for him to walk out of church, I wonder if this will always be my life. Dad says he wants a better future for me. He doesn't want me stepping up to run the club, but if anything happened to him, I know I wouldn't be able to walk away from the family who helped raise me.

I know Dad would much prefer it if I studied for a degree at some fancy ass school when I'm older. I doubt I could ever sit in an office or walk around in heels and a designer labelled outfit. It's not me. Instead, I'm the tomboy who'll walk around with inked up arms and riding a bike because that's what I've always known and come to love.

Everyone isn't the same, of course, but just from my short life experience, I've witnessed that the roughest looking people are usually the kindest. Being judged on your looks, on your outer appearance is something the men of the club deal with on a daily basis. At school, I'm the girl most kids stay away from because of my father. Some fear him, some respect him. But most don't know him like I do.

All I want to do is find where I belong. And live with people who *see* me. The friends I have made at school are lovely, but I don't have anyone close enough to call a best friend. So, instead of focusing on a circle of friends, I've allowed myself to work hard at my subjects.

I've been passionate about a few things in my life, but I've always been focused on getting lost in art. My favorite school trips always involve visiting museums. Being able to see what the masters created all those years ago is a privilege. It's how I want to be remembered.

When I'm eighteen, I'll train with the tattoo parlor who did all my dad's ink. I refuse to work in some suit and tie world where I don't belong. I'll be famous for my drawings one day.

I flick through my iPad that Dad got me for Christmas, and find the design I was working on a few days ago. There are so many intricate lines. I need to focus on the drawing, rather than what's going on around me.

Crossing my legs, I ignore the noise of the bar, and work on the dark lines on the screen instead. The clubhouse has always been a hive of activity. Even though I prefer the quiet, there's a sense of belonging in being so close to the family I grew up with. They may not be my blood, but they're loyal and they love me.

Each of the men my father rules over would die for me. It's as if I lost one mother and gained at least a dozen dads. Sometimes more when the other chapters visit. Being the daughter of a motorcycle club president comes with perks. But it also puts a damper on leading a normal life.

Most boys don't talk to me. Most are afraid. My friends all have boyfriends, but I've never even been kissed. My dad says it's a good thing because boys only hurt you in the end. But he's never hurt a woman in this club. He's never even punished me when I've done something wrong.

The clinking of glasses is soothing as the prospects get ready for a party tonight. Being of Irish descent, Dad always celebrates St. Patrick's Day with an all night drinking session. There'll be music, dancing, and hooking up—that's what the kids at school call it. I may not be entirely innocent. I've learned about the birds and bees from my friends, listening to the stories they tell me. Their folks sat them down when they turned twelve and explained what happens when a man and woman love each other. My father has avoided that chat with me, and if I'm honest with myself, I'm glad he has.

I'm far from considering having a boyfriend. Even though Lindsay, my best friend, has a boy she kisses sometimes, I find it all too emotional. She's constantly worried about her clothes and hair, while I love my short cropped, dark, spiky look.

I'm lost in thought, wondering what it would be like to have a boyfriend one day, when the doors finally open and the men file out. Some of them greet me, others ruffle my hair. I wanted it like my mama's, dark and super short. It's a boyish haircut, but I love it.

"Hey, Clover girl," Dad says as he nears me.

But I can't focus on my father, who's now staring at me. Instead, my gaze lands on the person behind him. It's a man I've never seen here before. He's standing half hidden, but it's as if he's taking up the entire room. As if he's sucked all the air from my lungs and stolen my breath.

He doesn't smile. He doesn't move. I force myself to look at my father and smile.

"Hey, Dad."

But when I glance back at the stranger, he's looking at the screen on my lap, staring at the design I've drawn. I quickly lock the device and stand. My dad pulls me into his arms and presses a kiss on the top of my head. He's always been affectionate, which is rather strange for a man who looks as scary as he does. With tattoos covering his arms and neck, and even a few on his hands, he gives off an air of danger.

"This is a good friend of mine from Ireland. He's going to be staying here for the party tonight," Dad tells me as he turns to look at the stranger. "Sully, this is the princess of the Kovenant." Dad is so proud of saying those words. He introduces me like that to everyone and anyone who'll listen.

I force myself to meet the intense stare of this man. Sully is certainly no boy. He must be in his mid-twenties at least. He looks much older than the young prospects who are hoping to patch into the club. He's got dark stubble on his jaw, as if he hasn't shaved in a few days. His hair is messy with soft curls at the nape of his neck.

I've seen handsome men before. Some are on posters stuck on my wall, mainly from rock bands of the eighties because my father introduced me to that genre of music. But this stranger is better looking than all those guys. He also looks like he's used to being stared at, but he's not boasting by being loud and annoying. He's not smiling, but he definitely doesn't seem bothered that I'm watching him.

He doesn't meet my eyes for a long while, but when he does, I see it. There's a darkness that seems to flicker in the orbs looking at me. He doesn't smile, only offers me a nod in greeting, and I'm disappointed I can't hear his accent. My father may be Irish, but he's lived here most of his life, so he doesn't have the lilt I've only ever heard on television.

"I need you to go to your room," my father whispers in my ear. "I'll call you when we're done and you can come down for pizza with the rest of the youngsters."

Since I was a child, Dad has always kept me at arm's length when it comes to the serious matters within the club. I am allowed in the bar area, but when there are meetings, or if something important is happening, I'm meant to stay in the main house. This time, it seems, it's no different.

"Okay." I drag the word out in frustration, and I'm pretty sure I notice a hint of a smile on the stranger's face. It's so small, I would have missed it if I wasn't staring at his lips.

I've never really had a crush on any of the boys at school, but this is no boy. Sully's tall, quiet, and dangerous, and I can't stop my heart from slamming against my ribs when he looks directly at me. His eyes seem to look right through me, as if he's seeing my soul.

As I make my way out of the bar, I glance over my shoulder one last time. If he's from Ireland, he may not be around for long, and I might never see him again. One last look. That's all I need. But it's the biggest mistake because he smiles back at me, and at that moment, I know I'll never forget the handsome stranger who stole my teenage heart.

When I get to my bedroom, I shut the door and flop onto my bed with my iPad beside me. My father doesn't know I listen in on his meetings. I do it because I want to make sure I know what's going on. If he's in danger, I have to know.

Enemies of the club are always threatening his life, so if he's walking into a situation where he could be hurt, I'd rather know beforehand. I've spent my short life preparing for the worst. I don't believe in fairy tales, thinking that happy ever afters happen. They don't. Stories with happy endings are nothing but pure fiction.

Even though I try my best to focus on the sketch

on the screen, I can't. All I can think about is the man downstairs. *Sully.* I whisper his name out loud, just once. And I decide I like the way it tastes on my lips. On my tongue.

I roll over onto my back and stare at the ceiling. I've ingrained the image of him in my mind. It's as if my brain took a snapshot, a forever photo, so I'll never forget what he looks like. I don't want to forget. Perhaps he's my first real crush.

I can't help but giggle, thinking about him kissing me. I'm only fifteen, and he must be at least twenty-five. That's a big difference. A man like him would never wait for a girl like me. That only happens in movies.

My life is no movie.

CHAPTER 3

The Present

She's naked in my bed, looking at me as if she's about to cry. It isn't stoppin' the beast from roarin' inside me. It wants out, it needs to know what the fuck this girl has gotten herself into. "What is it, Clover? Ye can tell me anythin', ye know that by now."

"He's going to come for me, and he's going to kill me." Her words slowly sink into my soul. The fact that

I'm already breakin' all my rules for her doesn't mean I can fight just how she makes me feel. It's wrong to want her as much as I do. It's feckin' bollocks to crave her like I do.

I'm not a gentle person, not by any means, but with her, I'm goin'ta have ta be. "What are ye talkin' about?"

"Do you remember me?" Her voice is a whisper of worry and pain. I want ta take all of that away and give her the happiness I know she deserves.

Before she can admit anythin' ta me, I say, "I know who you are, wee thing. I remember."

I don't think she expected me to confess ta that, because her eyes widen as she looks at me. If I had ta be honest, I didn't think I'd be tellin' her that either.

I'm now unsure of what ta say to her. Lookin' at Clover, I realise I've been blind all the time we've been together. But she looks so different from the young girl I met all those years ago. She's grown up, and her body's now a colourful canvas, rather than the smooth, porcelain skin I remember. Her tattoos may hide the scars of her past, but I see right through the ink. She can't hide from me.

"My ex," Clover mumbles. "He's going to come for me. And I'm not sure what to do alone." The fear in her tone, the break in her words as her voice cracks causes my chest ta tighten.

"Why didn't ye tell me when we were in that shitehole of a place?" I ask her.

When I first saw her sitting in the rehab centre, I didn't think anythin' of it. She was merely a pretty stranger ta me. But now I know who she is. Now that I'm lookin' at her, I can't believe she's real. All grown up. And there had to be a reason fer her to be in the rehab clinic, there had to be.

"Honestly, I don't know," Clover whispers as she shakes her head. "I didn't think I would ever need to tell you," she says before turnin' her gaze away from me. "I was struggling with addiction, taking painkillers when I didn't really need them. My past..." She shakes her head before she continues, "It's littered with violence, and I used to drown out the agony with pills."

"Tell me about him. I want ta know about that arsehole, I want a name," I order her, but I keep my voice low. I don't want ta scare her, but I want nothin' more than to force her ta look at me. I don't like the idea of her hurtin', but I know my life will only put her in more danger. The club life isn't fer her. She grew up inside a club, so she knows the dangers it brings.

"Rogan Hudson, but I know he used to use a different last name when he did jobs for the gangs he worked for, but that is something I was never privy to," she whispers, the tremble in her voice is enough to confirm she's afraid. "He's not a good person. And I have no doubt he will find me. He was the one who put me in hospital. I ran when I could, and I never wanted to look back. But I'm sure this is the calm before the storm."

"Ye shoulda left and never told me, darlin'," I inform her as I push away from the bed. "It's not safe fer ye with me, this world..." I look toward the window, not wantin' ta see the heartbreak in her expression at my words. "And the idea of someone hurtin' ye," I murmur. "That doesn't sit well with me."

I don't know if I can stop myself from claimin' her. Now I know who she is, the girl from all those years ago, but I know I can't taint her life with mine.

"Are you saying you *want* me to leave?" Dejection laces her words, her voice tight with annoyance and broken with sadness, and I don't feckin' blame her.

I can't face her, so I move to the window and look out over the city. The old warehouse where I live was turned into flats a long while ago. The moment I saw this place I knew I could find solace here.

I lean my forearms against the window. The sun's higher now. Its light streams through the panes. And that's when I feel her hand on my shoulder. Even the smallest, most tender touch sets me on edge. I didn't expect ta want her, but now she's found her way into my life, I don't know how ta push her away.

I don't want Clover to see the man I've become. And I can't tell her the truth about why I was in her home town all those years ago. Guilt sits in my gut like a lead weight as I turn my head to glance at her from over my shoulder.

Those pretty eyes stare up at me as she watches me fer a reaction. I don't know what she needs from me. She's the first woman ta look at me as if I'm a feckin' hero. It's been a long time since I've had a woman in my bed who I actually didn't mind wakin' up to the next mornin'. Those I've been with in the past always knew I was not goin'ta give them more than one night.

"Will you please let me in?" she asks in a tone that makes my chest tighten.

Feckin' hell. I can't do this. There's so much she doesn't know about me. I realise it's my own fault, but there isn't a way ta tell her the truth. Because if I do, she'll hate me forever. And perhaps that's not what I want.

"You shoulda never come here," I tell her. "It's not a place fer a wee thing like yerself."

"I am not a weak, helpless girl anymore," she spits out.

I don't blame her for being angry. I would be too if I were her. But then again, I don't mean to talk down to her. She's strong—I can see that. It's so feckin' clear to me. However, I'm more afraid of me hurtin' her than I am of anyone else hurtin' her.

"I didn't think ye were, darlin'." I shake my head as I regard her. "All I'm sayin' is there are things in my world that could hurt ye, and I wouldn't want that."

Clover drops her hand, and I finally take in her beauty. She's draped in only the sheet from the bed as she looks up at me.

"Don't let your fears take over and eclipse what we've found, Sully. I'm not scared of what life throws at me anymore. I'm made of stronger stuff," she tells me in that gentle accent that makes me smile.

"Then I best get ye into the shower," I say, but deep down, I'm still worried about hurtin' her.

It's not goin'ta be a straightforward journey, and her past doesn't afford much promise of happiness. She may be here fer an escape, but one thing I've learned about life, it will fuck ye when ye least expect it. And I've a feelin' the man she's been runnin' from will eventually find her.

"Will you be joining me, Sully?"

She arches a brow at me, those feckin' eyes callin' to me. But I've work ta do at the club. Also, I need to have Tye look into her past. I'm goin'ta have to find that bastard who hurt her before he finds her.

"I would love ta, but I've got some work that needs doin'," I tell her as I lean in to press my lips to hers. "Text me when ye're at work. I need to know ye're safe."

"I will." It's clear she's not happy. I can hear the excitement fadin' from her voice, but right now, I have ta focus on the task at hand.

Leavin' Clover is difficult, but as I swing my leg over my bike, I know it's fer the best. At least, it's what I think is best. I've not been in a relationship like this before, but now I am, I know I'm goin'ta have ta step up and be a man she can be proud of. I need to be her strength. Even though she may not need a hero, and I'm far from one, I have ta give her someone she can believe in.

That is, until she finds out the truth.

The thought makes me shudder as I pull out of the side street and make my way to the clubhouse. My mind is a feckin' mess as I consider just what I'm goin'ta have ta do when it comes to Clover. I'm not worried about killin' the fecker who hurt her, but it's the idea of goin' back ta see her family. She may have run, but she still needs to see them. She clearly knows all the implications of who she is—a princess of a biker club with links to far too many dangerous people.

When I met with Sean all those years ago, he asked me to find out about the mob. When I sent him the information about Bragan, he told me to keep clear of him. I didn't understand why, but then, not long after, the news hit me about Sean being killed by the Cartel. I was never able to delve into the reasons Sean had, but I trusted him, so I obeyed his command.

I know he had to fight for his territory, and that won't stop anytime soon. It's something they've always had to watch out fer. Their club is based on a mountain pass which makes it easy to invade. But their dealings in guns and ammo have made sure their territory can be overtaken if a new supplier can offer the same items cheaper.

And that's what happened.

When I pull up to the gates of the clubhouse, and make my way up the drive, I notice Monster and Rebel leaning against the wall. Rebel has a smoke hangin' from his lips. Their expressions are dire, and I wonder what the feck has happened now.

We're still searchin' for Bragan. Since he's gone underground, we've had every connection lookin' fer him. But there's been no luck.

"What's goin' on?" I ask as I step up to where the lads are standin'.

Monster looks over at me and shakes his head. "We had some intel on Bragan, but he's feckin' disappeared again. So, feckin' close, and the bastard's gone."

The anger in his tone is at an all-time high, and I know there's goin'ta come a time when it's goin'ta boil over. And when that day comes, all hell is goin'ta break loose. I wish we could find this fecker and put all this shite to bed.

"We will find him. There's no doubt about it. Ye want me to head to the warehouse?"

"Aye," Monster says as he pushes away from the wall. "We need a major clean up. While ye were with Clover, I had a couple of informants come forward. We have locations to more of Bragan's underground locations. I'll be flyin' out to London in a couple of days."

"And what do you want me to do?"

"Stay here, clean the warehouse, and make sure the club is looked after," Monster informs me. "Rebel is leavin' tonight for Amsterdam. So we'll have to have church before then. I want everyone on the same page. There can't be any feck ups."

"I need Tye to do some diggin' fer me as well," I say.

"There's someone I need to find."

"Does this have anythin' ta do with yer wee girlfriend?" Monster's stare pins me to the spot.

I nod. "Aye, when I met her in the rehab centre, I got the impression somethin' was wrong, and now I know, I'm going to find the bastard, and make him pay." I can't hold back the venom in my tone.

"Understood," Monster says with a hand on my shoulder, offerin' it a squeeze. "If you need anythin' else, the club is here. There's no need to be thinkin' ye're on yer own in this."

I've spent most of the time I've been at the club tryin'ta learn to ask fer help. There have been many times in my life where I've felt at odds with others gettin' too close to me. I tend to push people away. But I've come to realise it's only to the detriment of myself. And I can't afford ta put Clover in anymore danger. Even if I try ta do this alone, I know there'll be fallout for the club. I'm not sure how I know this, but I feel it in my bones.

"I appreciate that, Monster, I really feckin' do," I tell him.

"We're family," he responds, with no hint of a joke in his tone. "And that's what family members do. They stand by each other," Monster says as he offers me a nod and heads inside, leavin' me with Rebel.

"How are ye doin' with everythin'?" I ask him, knowing there are still tensions between him and Callia.

They've been skatin' around each other fer years, but he's never taken the plunge and told her how he feels. I figured somethin's gotta give eventually, but it hasn't yet. I wonder if it ever will. I can't judge his choices, though. My own decisions have been feckin' shite.

"Aye, not bad," he tells me. "But I'm still not trustin' Callia. I can't bring myself ta. I know who her da is, and it's messin' with my head." He looks at me, and I notice the pain in his expression.

"Shite happens, but ye can't blame Callia fer what her father, Bragan, has done, or even who the fecker is," I tell him. And it's true. If they judged me on my family, or connections, I'd never have a life. Can't say it's normal, but it's a life, nonetheless.

"Ye're right," Rebel tells me with a nod in agreement. "I just need ta figure out how the feckin' hell ta get over this block in my mind. She's in here now, and I don't want her to go," he says as he taps his forehead with his index finger, the new smoke he's just lit between his first two fingers.

"She'll always be there." And I can say that from

experience. It's not shite I'm spewin', it's the truth. "Thing is, ye got ta decide if she's worth it. Will you walk away and be content fer the rest of yer life? Or will ye fight fer the girl?"

"I guess we'll have ta wait and see what happens," he says.

The uncertainty is goin'ta mess with his head for a long while yet. You can't just walk away from somethin' and expect it ta disappear. Not when there's feelin's involved.

I make my way indoors to find Tye. He's got a lot of work to do fer me, and I want to get all the details as soon as possible. The clubhouse is quiet today. Usually it's packed with girls tryin'ta get the attention of the single brothers, but there's pure silence now. I find Tye at his computer when I walk into the office. He doesn't even look up as I enter the room. His focus is like a feckin' laser beam.

"Tye," I call to him, and only then does he lift his gaze to me. "What the feckin' hell are ye doin'?"

"I had a lock on Bragan's men, Also, he's been spotted in Amsterdam, so we're tryin'ta get ahead of the bastard." He leans back after finishin' up whatever he was typin' and looks at me. "What's up wit ye?"

"I need ye to do some diggin' fer me," I tell him.

"There's someone I need findin', but I have very little information about the arsehole." I pull out the name I've got written down on a piece of paper and slide it across to him. "Ye'll have te work with that."

He picks up the note and smiles. "Aye," he says. "I can do that."

He sets down the paper and beckons me round to the other side of his desk where the magic happens. He opens a browser and types in some feckin' numbers that make no sense to me, but he knows what he's doin'. I trust him.

If anyone can find this fecker, it's Tye.

"Leave it with me, I'll have somethin' fer ye in about twenty-four hours," he says before he once again is focused on his screen. With a nod, I head out. The warehouse needs my attention. If Monster's been interrogatin' someone, or a few someone's, I have a lot of work cut out fer me.

Once I'm on my bike, I start the engine, but before I can pull away, my phone buzzes in my pocket. Deep down, I know who it is, but I still smile when I see her name on my feckin' screen.

This is feckin' shite.

I can't be feelin' things fer her. She's still a stranger ta me. And she's also someone I can put in harm's way, which isn't somethin' I ever want ta do. Clover is different. I don't want ta let her get caught up in my world, but I'm not sure how I'm meant ta say goodbye to her. All I want is to keep her fer myself. I didn't expect ta find someone like her, but now she's here, I can't bring myself ta let her go.

Her message is brief, but it makes me grin. I don't smile, ever, but this girl, she's fecked with my heart and mind. And now she's goin'ta be mine. There's no longer a doubt in my mind, I'll do anythin' fer her. I'm already prepared ta kill fer her when I find the arsehole who hurt her. So, there's no longer any turnin' back on this.

Clover is mine, and lucky or not, she's goin' nowhere.

CHAPTER 4

Sully

When I walk into the warehouse, it's a feckin' mess. It looks as if there's been a war fought inside here, and there's blood on every feckin' surface. They've drenched the floor in deep red, and the bodies lie piled up on top of each other. Monster didn't tell me there were multiple corpses to deal with. But this isn't anythin' new ta me. I've been around death most of my life.

Sighin', I head over to the backroom to find my tools of the trade—a bucket of bleach and a mop that's brand new. I go through these things faster than a whore's knickers get dropped. But before I can do any actual cleanin', I need ta get rid of the bodies.

As I start ta work, my mind flits back to *that* night. The one moment I don't regret, but I still feel the guilt hittin' me right in the feckin' gut, and it knocks the wind from my lungs.

I've been out with mates all night, and I'm ready to fall into bed and sleep. Knackered doesn't even cover how I'm feelin' as I walk up ta the house. Ma has a wee bungalow on the outskirts of Belfast. It's where I grew up, and where I know Ma loves to be. She has her own wee garden outside, with pretty colourful flowers growin' in the summer, and in the winter, the frost eats away at the green, leavin' nothing but white when it snows.

It's late, nearin' midnight. The moon is full as I make my way up ta the front door. It's only when I unlock it with my key that I hear the crash inside. Without thinkin', I shove open the door and race into the house. The moment I step inside, I'm met with the dim light of the dining room bulb flickerin'.

"No!" There's a scream from Ma, which has me movin' without thinkin'.

My feet carry me up to the first floor landin' and that's

when I see him. Her arsehole of a boyfriend, Conall, has her down on the floor—one hand fistin' her hair, and the other poised in midair, ready to strike. But I'm faster than the drunken bastard.

I grip his wrist, and drag him away from Ma. I'm only fourteen, and he's older and got more bulk than me, but I don't give a shite. I've watched him hurt Ma fer far too long, and I'm done sittin' back and doin' nothin' about it. This fecker will die if I have anythin'ta do with it tonight.

"What the feckin' hell are ye doin' home?" His voice is filled with grit and anger, and his words are slurred as I pull away from him.

The bastard thinks I can't take him, but I know I can. I've been workin' out, I've been trainin' and I'll feckin' end his existence right feckin' now.

"Leave my ma alone, ye feckin' piece of shite," I bite out as my anger takes over. When I glance down at where Ma is tryin'ta stand, I notice she's bleedin' as she tries ta hold her nose which I now know is broken. But I can't lose focus now. This fecker will die tonight. It's a decision I make before I even know what I'm doin'.

Rage explodes through me when I see the crimson. My fists fly, and even though he tries to fight back, there's no stoppin' me. My knuckles are bloodied and raw, but I don't let up until he's nothin' more than a feckin' limp rag doll

I'm holdin' onto. I grip the bastard by his shirt collar, and I practically drag him down the stairs.

"Sully," Ma calls to me, but even though I hear her voice, I don't stop.

I'm happy she's alive and movin', but all that I can think about right now is makin' this arsehole pay for what he's done.

Where we live is a quiet cul-de-sac. It has a park hidden at the end of the road, which is exactly where I drag this fecker. He's tryin'ta fight me, but he's not strong enough. I'm runnin' on adrenaline, and nothin' can stop me. My mind is totally focused on killin' this arsehole right now. If I succeed, I'll have no feckin' guilt about it.

We reach the park, and I'm shakin' with rage. Ma is followin' behind, and I glance over my shoulder at her.

"Go back inside, Ma," I order, and it's the first time I've spoken to her like this.

All my life, I've been the obedient son she wanted, but right now, I'm far from that. I feel so removed from the man she's raised.

"Sully," she calls to me when I reach the swings. but I ignore her, my focus solely on the shite who harmed her. He's the only thing I need to focus on right now.

I shove the bastard onto one of the small, wooden seats. Then I grab hold of the swing chains, and I wrap them around his body and arms to keep him in place. I lean in so close, he can't look away from me. His nose is bloodied and broken, and I can't stop the smile from creasin' my face.

"You're goin'ta pay tonight," I tell him. It's a promise. A feckin' vow.

Fer years, I've spent my time watchin' him hurt my ma, and this time, I'm done. I won't ever again step away when I see a woman bein' hurt. Growin' up, I wanted to do somethin' about it, but I never could. I wasn't strong enough. Now I'm grown up, and there's no stoppin' me anymore.

My ma raised me to be a gentleman, but watchin' her suffer over the years has made sure I'm tougher than she ever thought possible. And I'm goin'ta use that tonight. She'll be free soon, and when she is, I know she'll finally get to enjoy her life. When I was growin' up, there were times she would pull me to the side and tell me to be a good man and never hurt a woman. This is fer her.

I pull the knife from my shoulder holster and hold it up so the fecker can see that tonight is the last time he'll ever touch any woman.

"Sully," Ma calls to me, stepping up to where I'm kneelin' in front of the arsehole who's still chained to the swing seat. "Don't do somethin' ye'll regret fer the rest of yer life, son."

"Ma," I say. "This is somethin' I'll never feckin' regret. You deserve far better than ye're gettin'. It's up to me now to look *after ye. So please," I tell her. "Go back inside, and I'll be with you when I'm done here."*

Our gazes lock for a long moment, and I half expect her to stop me. But then I notice her wince when she leans in to press a kiss to the top of my head.

"Be careful," is all she whispers before she leaves me with the man who's bound before me. He's lookin' at me with a smirk curlin' his lips, and anger takes ahold of me once more.

I lift the blade and grab his face, so he can't move, and I slowly slice a Joker type smile into each corner of his mouth. His cheeks are now a waterfall of crimson as he cries out in agony. Even his cries make me smile. Perhaps I'm no better than the bastard I want ta kill, but there's one difference between us—I'll never harm someone who's innocent. I don't hurt women or children, but arseholes like him, I'll gladly slice into tiny feckin' pieces.

I sit back and watch my handy work for a long while. My mind is filled with the image of him dying. I'm lost in the red drippin' from his pale skin. I don't stop, though, because once he's calmed down, I continue slicing his flesh, from under his eye down his left cheek. I want ta watch the fecker bleed out in front of me.

Keeping my stare on his, I smile. "Do ye think hurtin' innocent women makes ye a powerful man?" I ask him as I take the blade and slowly press it against his palm. His wrist is twisted and still bound in metal chains. He's not goin' anywhere any time soon. "In my books, that makes ye a feckin' coward."

"Ye think bein' a strong man is goin'ta get ye anythin' more than a lifelong sentence in the chokey? They'll lock ye up for this and leave ye in there until ye're old and grey. And who's gonna look after yer ma then?"

I know he's tryin'ta bait me, but I can't stop myself from raisin' the knife and slamming the handle into his face. There's a crunch in the moment of impact, and I smile once more. He needs to pay, and I'll gladly make sure he does.

"If ye think ye're a stronger man than I am," I tell him as I lean in and press the tip of the blade against his neck. "Then ye're mistaken because a real man, a strong feckin' man, would never hurt those who are weaker than him."

This time, I do smile. I laugh out loud while I listen to him gurgle as the metallic fluid from the wounds on his face slowly drips into his mouth and down the back of his. I wish we were at the Royal Bastards' warehouse. If we were, I'd ensure this arsehole was sent to hell with wounds he'd never fuckin' forget. But I'm goin'ta have ta make do with the blade and my bare hands.

"One day," he tells me. "When ye're all grown up and a real man, ye'll fall in love." His words make me laugh out loud because I know I'll never put a woman through the pain of spendin' her life with me. "Then ye'll realise they all need ta be handled in a certain way. Possessin' an obedient woman is the only way ye'll be happy."

"I'm not a feckin' monster," I yell at him as I drop the knife, and wrapping my hands around his neck, I squeeze until the light leaves his eyes and I finally end his life.

There's a certain power that comes with killin' a man. I can't deny it—I enjoyed it. I didn't think I'd ever find pleasure in being violent, but I shouldn't be surprised by it. I've grown up in a city that's shown me just how cruel real life is. With violence and cruelty a norm from a very young age. Despite Ma tryin'ta keep me from it, there is no escapin' the gangs in Belfast.

Soon, I'm hoping to be patched into my best friend's motorcycle club. I'll be part of a family I never thought I'd ever have. All my life, it's been only me and Ma, but now, I will have brothers who'll be there fer me whenever I need them.

I'm done.

He's gone.

I look down at the man I've just killed. Over the past few weeks, I've been cleanin' up for the club, but now I've taken a life, and there's no goin' back.

"You're not too bad at that." A deep voice comes from behind me and there's a chill that runs down my spine. I didn't think I'd be caught out here in the dark, but I shoulda known there's always someone watchin'. Especially when ye're doin' somethin' ye shouldn't be.

I turn to find a man from my past. He's a member of the IRA, an organisation I don't want anythin'ta do with. But with him as a witness, there's no doubt he's goin'ta want somethin' from me.

"What is it ye're wantin', Ronan'?" I bite out as I look at McCallum.

He's the da of Cormac, a guy I knew in school. I haven't seen Cormie in a few months, but I know he works fer his da now, doin' things I don't want to know about because it ain't good. Ronan McCallum is one of the few men I didn't want ta see while in this compromisin' position. I know he's not goin'ta let it go. And that's what worries me.

"It looks like ye're needin' some help," he tells me as he moves closer.

There's no hidin' the dead man in the swings, and there's no denyin' his life ended by my hand.

"I don't need help from the IRA," I tell him, but even as I say it, I know it's no use.

These feckers know everythin' that goes on in the city and indeed the country. There's no point in tryin' to hide this— he's already seen me. There's no denyin' what I've done, and I know Ronan will never let this go. He likes'ta have *somethin'ta hold over people.*

I should've done the killin' in the house, but I didn't want Ma to witness it. And I didn't need her cleanin' up my mess.

Ronan steps up to me and lands a hand on my shoulder. Now I know I'm in shite. "I'm here, Sully, and I'll make sure this goes away."

"What's yer price?" I ask him as I glance over my shoulder.

"Ye'll clear yer debt by helpin' out when I need ye," he tells me, and I almost sag in relief because he doesn't immediately ask me to kill someone, but I know it will be a short-lived reprieve.

Fer a long moment, I wonder if it's worth it. If I accept this deal, I know I'll live my life worried fer when he's goin'ta collect. But if I refuse, I don't know how to get rid of this body. All my experience of cleanin' is in the warehouse.

I'm in shite either way, so I look at Ronan McCallum and nod. "Aye," I say after far too feckin' long. "I'll do whatever it is ye're needin'."

"Ye have ta remember though, Sully," Ronan tells me as he looks at me. "After doin' this fer ye today, I can call on ye any time, any day. There isn't any expiry date." And I realise I've just sold my soul to the devil. And there's no goin' back.

It was a long time ago, but I still would do the same again. There's never been a time I regretted what I did.

Ma's boyfriend deserved to die, and I'm proud to say I was the one who did it. But the problem is, the past is comin' back ta bite me in the arse, and I can't have that. Not with Clover in my life now. I can't put her in danger—that's somethin' I'll never allow. If anythin' happens ta her, I'll never forgive myself.

CHAPTER 5

The Past

It's been a long day, and all I want to do is get into a hot bath, relax with a book, and not do much else. But even though I've been working for most of the day, the moment I walk into the house, I have to ensure dinner is started and on the stove.

I always have to be available when he needs me. It doesn't matter what I've been doing all day, it's up to him to tell me what I'm feeling.

Rogan is the man of the house, and he likes to remind me that he prefers things said and done in a certain way. He hasn't always been like this, but now, a year into our relationship, things have changed. He's become a stranger to me, and even though I still love him, something dark has taken over him.

We met at a bar one night just after Dad died. I was seventeen at the time, and still hurting from losing my father. Rogan knew a few of the men from the Kovenant motorcycle club. He was charming, friendly, and he stole a kiss when the guys weren't looking. I was enamored with him—his buzz cut, dark hair, the stubble that covered his angular jaw, and his deep chocolate eyes that shimmered with amusement when he looked down at me. All the things I found attractive drew me in quickly, and soon I was moving in with him.

It didn't matter that he was much older. He treated me like an equal and made me feel as if my opinions mattered, so instead of moving slowly, I raced into love.

He hasn't said the word to me yet, but I know he feels it just as deeply as I do in my heart because there are times I glimpse that emotion shining in his eyes.

But then he goes out drinking with the guys from the club and comes home angry.

He doesn't like me going out alone. I used to think it was him being protective, but now I realize he's just trying to keep me under his thumb. When I finally landed a job, he said he was happy, but it soon turned sour when he started to belittle me.

The rumble of engines outside alerts me that he's home. My stomach twists. Cold fear skitters down my spine and it feels like ice has entered my veins. It's enough to send any sane person mad. The darkness that consumes me when I hear his boots on the stairs makes my vision blurry. I'm not sure if he's sober or not, but when the front door opens and I hear the sound of his keys jingling as they land in the bowl at the entrance to our apartment, I pray.

I've never been one to seek help from a higher power. I don't think belief in a deity that can save you should carry you through life. But right now, all I can do is pray.

"Clover." His deep, rumbling tone rattles me as he enters the kitchen to find me at the hob.

The food I'm preparing will need some time to simmer. I turn to offer him a smile, but stop myself when I see the violence in his gaze.

"I was out with the guys," he tells me. "We went down to the bar for lunch and had some drinks."

That's telltale confirmation that tonight is going to go one of two ways—either he'll get angry, or he'll pass out. I pray for the latter.

"Did you have a good time, then?" I plaster a fake smile on my face. Deep down, I hope he won't lose his shit with me. My mind is whirring with possibilities of how I can calm him down.

"I was, until I found some asshole who said he knows you," he informs me as his tone becomes aggressive.

That's when my stomach sinks right down to my feet. I didn't expect this evening to go well when he walked in and he said he'd been out with the guys, but this is something different.

"What?" My voice is a whisper, fear clearly lacing the word as I say it.

"You heard me," Rogan responds as he pulls the fridge door open and finds a beer. The pop of the can echoes in my ears, causing me to cower back. I don't want to get into an argument, but it seems as if he's ready for one.

"I don't know what you're talking about, Rogan." The moment the words leave my mouth, he spins on his heel and the open can of beer is flying across the room toward me.

I manage to move out of the way, and thankfully, it misses me and hits the wall. But the spray spurts from the can and empties all over the floor behind me. I can see a late night of cleaning is in my future. The sticky liquid will soon dry, and it will be a nightmare to get it out from between the floorboards. And if I don't succeed, I'll be chastised like a child. Told I'm no good at anything once more. I've become accustomed to it now, and I believe it when he says it.

"I don't like the fact you're whoring yourself out with random men, and I don't fucking like it when they're out there boasting about you," he spits, anger drenching every word.

"I wasn't *whoring* myself out," I bite out, and I know, the moment the words are out of my mouth, it's a mistake to think I can fight back when he's in this kind of mood.

"Then who the fuck is Cody?" His eyes blaze with rage as he glares at me.

He nears me, and I instinctively step back until I hit the wall. Now there's nowhere else to go, and I wait for the moment of impact.

There have been moments in my life where I've wondered why I was put here. Even as a young child, I was philosophical, asking Dad about why we lost Mom and why her life was shorter than his.

Things like that always made me wonder about heaven and hell. We're taught to believe they exist, even though there's no proof we end up in either place when we die.

Right at this moment, as Rogan's hand grips my arm and drags me out of the kitchen, I wonder if hell is *actually* real. It could be this moment I'm living now, but the blazing inferno could also be my whole relationship with Rogan. A daily occurrence of me paying for sins I don't know anything about.

I'm nothing more than a shadow, a ghost of who I was. Perhaps I'm the one who's dead, and those I love—Mama and Dad—are still breathing. Maybe they're the ones mourning me.

Rogan shoves me into the bedroom where I stumble to my knees. I quickly scurry to the far corner of the room we used to make love in, but it's no longer like that. There are no tender moments, no soft touches. Those disappeared along with the Rogan I fell in love with a long time ago, and in his place is the man before me—rough, violent, angry.

The wall at my back is the only thing keeping me from running. I'm cornered. A mouse shaking as the predator makes its way closer. Rogan's strong hand grips my neck, his fingers tightening around the column as he squeezes the air from my lungs. If I panic, it will only make things worse, so I try to inhale through my nostrils.

"Do you think you can go fucking around, and I won't find out?" he demands.

His jealousy only started when I told him about my job. Before that, he wasn't like this. I don't want to make excuses for him. I used to, but not anymore. There's no denying I'm in a dangerous situation, and I should have walked out months ago.

I used to get angry when I heard about women in relationships like mine. I would wonder why the hell they stayed, but it's so hard to walk away. It's only now I finally I get it. I'm the one I should be angry with.

The fist that makes contact with my stomach has me doubling over, and then he steps back, those dark eyes filled with anger. He grips my hair, tangling his fingers in the strands, and he drags me over to the bed where I know the worst is yet to come.

"Please, Rogan. I've done nothing wrong," I try to reason with him, to explain I'm innocent of the things he's accusing me of, but it's no use.

He holds me face down on top of the covers. The

soft material does nothing to soothe me. The roughness of his other hand as he rips my leggings down over my hips causes me to cry out. And that's when I hear his belt being removed. The sound of his buckle echoes in my ears. It's like the clanging of a church bell, only the sound isn't leading me to salvation, and I'm not in the quiet solace of a cathedral.

It's a warning of the agony about to be bestowed on me. The first lash of pain has me trying to claw myself away from him, but his firm grip on my head is too fierce.

A second fiery bite of pain stings through me. My flesh is burning, and even as I scream, the mattress muffles the sound. Again and again, the leather licks at my body. He attacks not only my ass but also my thighs and back.

By the time the final blow comes, I'm close to passing out. The fight has left my body and my fingers no longer grip the material of the blankets on our bed. Even though I hear the belt hit the carpet with a soft thud, I know it's not over.

"Do you see what you make me do?" Rogan whispers as his zipper hisses.

This is what always happens after. He drags me up the bed and turns me onto my back. It causes me to cry out as the blankets touch my open wounds, sending fire and ice racing through me. It's like being burned. You don't realize just how painful it is until it sinks into your brain and steals your breath.

I'm weakened. I can't fight, and he knows it. This is how he prefers me. Nothing more than a broken toy for him to play with. For him to abuse as he wishes.

When he finally thrusts inside me, the agony is profound. I'm not ready for him, but he doesn't care. There's no longer any love or affection in this man. Something almost demonic has taken all the good I once saw in his eyes.

"Please, stop," I beg, but Rogan doesn't hear me. He can't because he's possessed by whatever the fuck has ahold of his soul.

His hands on my shoulders force me down, and the full weight of him pins me to the bed. His cock feels like sandpaper sliding into me, the softness of my body far from wet, far from accepting. Using my palms, I try to lift him off me, but he's too heavy, too strong.

The grunts that rumble through him make me feel ill. I want to puke. I can feel the bile rising into my throat. The acidic burn is the only way I know I'm still awake, that I'm still alive. Turning my head, I cough out the liquid that spills from my lips.

"Fucking filthy slut," Rogan spews. "You should be thankful I'm even showing you affection." His hand comes into contact with my cheek, causing stars to dot my vision.

More smacks follow, one after the other. He doesn't stop until I taste the familiar flavor of metal. I'm sure I'm going to pass out from the loss of blood. Once he's finished, I hear his sigh of contentment as he moves off me, and I'm finally able to breathe again.

"Best be checking on dinner," Rogan tells me as he zips up his jeans and leaves me on the bed.

I know I had the stove on low, but I'm pretty sure dinner is ruined now. Forcing myself to move, I don't bother righting my clothes he'd ripped from me. Instead, I find the soft material of my beach wrap and tie it around me. I don't dare touch my butt because I know it will only cause more agony.

In the kitchen, I flick off everything, thankful that nothing is burned too badly. He won't notice because he won't eat. The sound of a glass tumbler from the living room of a drink being poured is the only evidence I need to know he's not interested in what I've made. He's still drinking, which means he'll soon be passed out in the armchair with the television blaring.

My torture for today is complete, and I'm able to

shower and try to clean myself. The cool water doesn't really soothe me, but it washes away the blood. With every movement, I feel him. It's why he does it—to remind me of who I belong to. He needs me to know that no matter where I am, or who I'm with, I will always be his. That's what he told me the first time it happened.

Leaning against the cold tiles, I close my eyes and try to calm my constantly erratic pulse. But that's when the shattering of glass startles me, and I slip to the floor with my eyes snapping open in surprise. The shower door is in pieces around me. Smaller shards cut into my skin.

Rogan's boot is already closing in, and it slams into my ribs.

"Fucking little bitch. The food is burned."

His words no longer unravel me, because my vision is beginning to blur. I blink a few times, but I can no longer see him clearly. Everything goes cloudy, as if I'm in a steamy tunnel. There's nothing I can focus on. And then, everything goes black.

CHAPTER 6

The Present

When I finally get home, I find the apartment empty. I'm pretty sure Clover is still at the pub, which means I can clean up and head down there. She's been on my mind all day. Even though I'm still waitin' on Tye ta get back to me with intel, I'm goin'ta go see my girl. I haven't told her what I'm doin', and I don't think she'll be happy when she finds out, but I have to do it. There's no way for me to ignore the fact she's mine, and I'm not goin'ta have her live in fear of that bastard findin' her.

In the bathroom, I strip down and step into the shower before turnin' on the taps. Icy water hits my back, causin' me ta wince. As it warms, I lather up ta get the stench of death from my skin. But I know, no matter what I do, it will always be there. I can't change the fact I've killed in the past and I'm a cleaner for a motorcycle club, so I'll never be rid of the blood on my hands.

Once I'm done, I head into the bedroom and get ready to go out. The pub isn't far from my home, and it still surprises me, after all these years, I'd never actually been inside until the night I found Clover there. The guys always told me it wasn't a bad place ta get a good pint a Guinness, but I never bothered goin' in, preferrin' to drink alone in my flat or at the club instead.

With spring on the way, the weather is slowly changin'. I don't like hot weather, but thankfully, we've had some mild summers over the past few years.

"Sully."

My name is called, and I turn to find an old acquaintance that I'd rather not introduce to Clover.

"Been a wee while, Cormie," I greet, offerin' him a smile, but it's a plastered on expression in the hopes of gettin' rid of him quickly.

"I hear ye're still ridin' wit the Bastards," he tells me. It's something everyone knows.

Belfast may be a city with a large population, but people know what goes on, especially when it comes ta those they deem are either breakin' the law or aren't doing what they should be doin'. The Bastards have their reputation to uphold in the city, and they do it well.

"Aye, what's it to ye?" My gut churns with annoyance and frustration.

He's one part of my past I wanted to leave behind. When I walked away from that life, from the gang, I never turned back. Ronan may have helped me out of a sticky situation, but he wanted my soul in return. I had to do jobs fer him. When he witnessed how ruthless I was at such a young age, he knew he could exploit it. I was a slave to him because I didn't want anyone findin' out what I'd done—killed someone with my bare hands.

And when I started workin' fer Ronan, I got in deep. My focus was solely on keepin' my name out of his mouth, so he didn't tell the police about my actions.

And that's when I befriended Cormie. We became as close as brothers. But there was never any loyalty between us. I learned that the life of a gang member was nothin' more than a waitin' game to when you die.

Every illegal thing I did was another strike against my name. I waited fer the feckin' Reaper ta come fer me. Deep down, I wanted him ta take me away. But he never did, and I realized I had ta make the choice to walk away, or live a life I hated.

There was even a time I considered leavin' the country, but I knew I was never goin'ta be able to live anywhere else. Ireland was in my blood, and Belfast was a part of me, one I was never goin'ta get out of my system. And I didn't want rid of it. All I wanted was a fresh start. That's what Monster gave me.

"My Da wants to know if you'd be willin' ta help us out with somethin'." He offers me a grin that isn't at all friendly.

Cormac McCallum is not a good'un. He's a feckin' bastard who'll kill anythin' as long he's followin' orders. Since joinin' the IRA, he doesn't give a shite about the lives he's stealin'. He takes after his da, Ronan, walkin' in the shoes of the men who tore this country apart.

There are so many things I don't know about him anymore. When we were mates, we told each other everythin', things have changed. And if I had to be honest with myself, I prefer it that way. If I agree to help him, he might learn to trust me again, but I won't. I'm not goin' back ta that life.

The idea of havin'ta answer ta Ronan again makes me feel sick to my stomach. I may have helped him out with jobs in the past, but I'm not the same person anymore. When Monster gave me a place to belong, I turned my life around. Granted, I still do shite fer the club, cleanin' up after the interrogations we do, but I no longer deal in illegal shite. No drugs, no guns. And it's a part of my life I don't want to remember.

"Not anytime soon. I'm busy, wee man," I tell him. "I don't have the time or the resources ta get back into that." I'm hopin' that's the end of it. All I need right now is a drink and ta see my wee woman. But I know he isn't goin'ta let me walk away so easily.

"You know, me da helped ye when ye needed it," he reminds me easily. I didn't think he'd bring that up, but I'm also not surprised.

"Aye," I tell him with a nod. "But times have changed. Things have moved on." Even though I doubt the reminder will deter this arsehole, I can't help but try.

He steps up to me, and I'm on full alert. I'm

unarmed, and I'm pretty sure he's carryin' a knife or maybe somethin' even more deadly. If it's a blade, I can fend him off, but if he has a gun, I don't stand a chance.

"I think ye should reconsider, Sully," he tells me. The earnest tone of his voice doesn't hide the malice hidin' under the surface. It's not him suggestin' anythin', it's him informin' me I don't have a choice in the matter.

He took all I had to give, and when I finally walked away, I told him I'd never work fer him again. What I did fer Ronan was over when I finally found a home with the club. When I agreed to obey McCallum, I was a wee boy, fourteen, but five years later, I knew I had to get out. I'd seen too many of my mates lying dead in the streets. Violence had become second nature. I didn't want that fer myself.

Monster doesn't know about what happened. None of the brothers knows. And I don't know if I can ever tell any of them why I left home at fourteen. Ma didn't want me around. She was angry with me fer what I'd done. Not because that bastard was dead, but she hated that I had given my life to Ronan by killin' Conall.

"Aye, well then, I suppose I don't have a choice in the matter," I tell Cormac. "What is it yer needin'?"

"Word around town is there's an undercover agent workin' with the police," he tells me. "Apparently it's a

wee lass who's tryin'ta suss out where the mob is hidin'
Bragan."

I almost laugh at how stupid that sounds. There have
been many battles between the mob and the coppers,
and nothin' ever came of it but death. Why would an
agent be interested in comin' all the way over here ta
take down the Irish mob?

"We need to find Bragan before the agent does,"
Cormie says then, draggin' my attention back to the
present. "Tell me ye and yer boyos will help us. There'll
be a pretty penny in it fer ye, mate."

"I'll see what I can do, but I ain't promisin' ye
anythin'. If we don't find the fecker, then we don't. I
don't need to be walkin' around with a target on my
head."

This time, I'm the one offerin' a threat behind my
words. I'm exhausted, and I'm done playin' games. This
has ta end at some point, and it has ta end here. They
may have somethin' te blackmail me with, but I'm sure
I can figure out a way to remove that. The thought
lingers fer a moment, and I wonder if I can talk to
Tye and see if he's able to erase that part of my past.
But goin' to him means I'm goin'ta have ta tell Monster
about what I did.

"Make sure ye sort it out fer us," Cormie tells me

before he spins on his heel and disappears into the night.

I don't need to ask him how ta get in touch. He'll be the one who'll track me down ta get the answers he wants. And that's a day I'm really not lookin' forward ta.

I need ta tell Clover I'm tryin'ta find Rogan, but I need to know she's safe. I can't go on knowin' she's livin' in fear, even if she walks away from this thing between us. If she does decide to leave, to pursue her art career, then I'm not goin'ta stop her. She deserves better than what I can give her. She should have a normal life, not workin' in some old pub in Belfast.

It's where I find Clover servin' a couple of lads who seem to be less than sober, but they're not givin' her any shite, which sets me at ease. I settle into a seat by the bar before she notices me. She's more focused on pullin' pints than seein' who's comin' in.

When her eyes meet mine, I recognise the glimmer of excitement that comes when someone's in love. Deep down, I wonder if I'm it fer her. We haven't said those words yet, but I know she feels it. It's so clear in her stare. And I wonder if I look at her the same way.

"How was yer day?" I ask as she pours me a Jameson and slides the glass over the counter towards me.

Her gaze flicks over to the rest of the bar before she answers, "It's been busy. I'm ready to get into bed and close my eyes." She offers me a smile, but there's somethin' in the way her mouth tilts downwards after, and the tension in her hand as she grips the bottle. There's a slight tremble I notice before she sets the whiskey down.

She lifts her eyes, and she's lookin' straight at me I can tell there's something she's hidin'. I want to push, to ask her what it is, but I don't. But deep down, I know she's not goin'ta tell me anythin' here. Once we're alone, I'll get it out of her. It hasn't been that long we've been together, but I can read Clover like a book. Those small tellin' signs when she's stressed are obvious to me now. I'm intrigued by her, how she can focus on work, on servin' drinks, while her mind is so clearly filled with worry. Perhaps she's heard from Rogan, but if she did, she would'a told me, I'm sure of it.

"Are you okay?" Clover watches me as she wipes down the bar, and I know I'm goin'ta have ta tell her all my secrets soon. The deeper I find myself fallin' fer this girl, the more I realise I can't hide forever. If I want her in my life, I'm goin'ta need to learn how to be honest and open about things. Even if they're not good. Even if I risk losin' her. I don't want somethin' based on lies.

It's the one thing I'm not willin' to accept.

My past has been littered with shite I should have never done. I know I shouldn't bring her into the darkness with me, but I also can't let her go. So, I'm going to have ta tell her the truth and let her decide.

"Aye," I tell her before I swallow back my drink. "Tonight, we're goin'ta have ta talk about a few things."

Her eyes widen in surprise at my words. "That sounds rather ominous."

"Nothing ominous at all," I say. "Just need ye ta know what past demons linger around me. I don't want ye stayin' with me when ye don't know the real man behind all the bullshit."

"You know I'm not going anywhere," Clover insists.

She's said it before, but I don't know how much of my past she knew back then. She only met me briefly when she was a teen. And even when we connected again in the rehab centre, I didn't give her the entire story. I couldn't tell her everythin'. I couldn't tell her just how much I loved killin' Ma's boyfriend.

"Aye, ye say that now, but I need ye ta know me. I want ye ta learn who I really am. And the only way ta do that is by tellin' ye the whole story. Everythin'. Even the darkest of shite."

·Clover sighs, but she nods slowly. "Fine. We'll sit

down tonight, and you can tell me everything you need to. And I guess I'll end up admitting a lot of my own truths as well."

"I want that," I tell her as I capture her hand in mine. There's nothin' I want more than ta have her be mine, fully. I sound like a feckin' lovesick arsehole right now. Monster would have a feckin' laugh if he were here listenin' ta me. "This won't work otherwise."

"You know, Sully," Clover says as she rounds the bar, the last customer havin' left, and stops next to me. "For a big, bad biker, you're a teddy bear when it comes to me."

"Aye, there's no doubt you make me weak, which is why I need ye ta know about my past. There are and will always be people comin' fer me. Wantin' to get somethin' from me. And I need ye ta be aware of it. Belfast may be a beautiful city, but it's a feckin' dangerous one."

I help her clean up, grabbin' glasses from the tables and wipin' down surfaces. I flick the lights off, leavin' us with only the small downlights illuminatin' the bar.

"I've spent my life in dangerous situations, Sully," Clover tells me when I'm once again settled on a stool watchin' her pack the last few clean glasses onto the shelves.

"I want ye ta tell me all about that bastard," I say to her because I need ta tell her what I asked Tye to do. "When I went to the club this mornin', I spoke to Tye."

"What? Why?" She knows who he is and what he does fer the club. There's no hidin'. She's pissed off at me.

"I want ta make sure ye're never goin'ta have ta look over your shoulder again." Even though I can tell she's angry I went behind her back, she must realise it's fer the best. She needs to be able to walk down the street without worryin' about that arsehole comin' after her.

"So you're going to look for Rogan, and then what? Kill him?" Her question may be a joke, but the look in my eye must tell her how serious I am because she freezes. "Sully—"

"You can't say anythin' ta change my mind, Lucky," I say to her. "The fecker will pay, and I'm goin'ta make sure ye're there to see it. You have to know what this life entails, and you also need closure."

"But killing someone isn't on my list of things to do before I die." Clover's cheeky response makes me chuckle. "I'm serious."

Even though I'm laughin', I know she's not goin'ta let this go. But she needs ta get her revenge. And I won't stop until Clover is healed.

I may not be a hero, but I'll make damn sure she's saved.

CHAPTER 7

I'm nervous.

That's the understatement of the year. I didn't expect Sully to want to talk, but I also want nothing more than to learn about his past. I've only gotten glimpses. And I'm sure those didn't fully explain what he's been through. I also want to tell him everything about my past. Even though he knows more or less what happened, there are things I have kept to myself. There are horrors I faced that I'm not entirely sure I'm strong enough to share.

But, if I'm planning on going to therapy, I need to dive right into those dark abusive parts of my life and make sure I'm able to revisit those memories and heal from them. I want to move forward with Sully. The future is us together, and I don't want to jeopardize that by hiding things from him.

I've learned all too well that when you hide parts of yourself, you're only hurting those who love you. And I'm sure Sully loves me. A man doesn't plan to kill someone just because he wants to get into a woman's pants.

Our feelings for are becoming clearer. But I do know there are things Sully hasn't told me. He wants to hurt Rogan, probably kill him for hurting me, and I'm sure there is more to it. He must have a definitive reason as to why he's so adamant, it can't just be his feelings for me.

When we get into his apartment, he flicks on the lights, and the enormous lounge and kitchen area illuminates in a soft yellow glow. There's a calmness to his home, and it feels safe to be here. I've not lived with another person in a while. When I left the rehab centre, I was on my own. And while it was good, there was always this hint of fear that held me hostage because I was convinced I'd be found.

Rogan has connections all over, especially with the motorcycle clubs. And while I don't know if he knows about the Royal Bastards, it won't be difficult for him to garner that information. As much as he's an asshole, he's crafty and will find out where I am eventually.

"Drink?" Sully ask as he turns to look at me from over his shoulder.

The fridge lights up his face as he watches my movements.

"Just water," I reply as I settle on the sofa, sinking into the cushions as I sigh the day away. It's been busy at work, my feet are sore, and all I want is to sleep, but this is important.

When Sully joins me, he's holding a bottle of beer, and he hands me a glass of chilled water from the fridge. He sits beside me, facing me, and I turn to look at him. We've been sat on these cushions so many times before, but tonight it feels different. There's more to this than just a couple enjoying time alone together.

"So, do you want to start, or would you like me to go first?" I ask him as I swig back the cool liquid.

Sully is silent for a long moment before he says, "When I was younger, it was just me and Ma. There were so many times over the years I wanted to give her a beautiful house. I wanted ta buy it so she never had to run again."

His tone is dire, and my stomach twists with what's coming next. I know this is difficult for him to talk about because he's told me some of it before. But tonight, we're going to dive even deeper.

"She was seein' this arsehole fer a wee while. I was ten when he first came ta the house. A wee scrawny lad who didn't know how ta fight. I was a kid who only had his mother to raise him. But the moment Conall walked into the house, I knew I would never call him Da. I hated him from the second I saw him. Somethin' about him just didn't sit right with me."

"I can't picture you as a skinny, young boy," I whisper with a small smile on my lips.

Sully is over six-foot, with broad shoulders, long wavy hair, and a beard. He looks like a Viking, rather than the child he's describing to me now.

"Aye, I was a runner. Kept me skinny fer a long while. But one night I woke up, heard them fightin' and I got up out of bed. The floorboards were on my side that day—they didn't creak as I made my way out of my bedroom and into the hallway. Ma and Conall were downstairs, and they were arguin' about money. He'd taken some of her savin's and used it fer gamblin' debts. By then, he'd been around fer a couple years."

"And he was staying with you?"

Sully nods. "Aye, fer the most part. There were nights he wouldn't come home, which were the nights I was happiest. But I knew he was out fuckin' whores in the city. Ma didn't want ta believe it, but it was true. I'd heard the whispers about the bastard."

My chest tightens when I take in the look on Sully's face. There's a darkness in his eyes, a rage that I know will never be gone. He hated the man in question, and I've no doubt now about what happened to him. But I don't interrupt Sully's story.

"That night I watched as the cunt hit Ma across the face. I saw red. There wasn't anythin' that could stop me from racin' down those stairs and gettin' in a hit of my own. My fist slammed into his back, and I lost all control. I kept hittin' him, but the bastard was big, much bigger than me. And he punched me, knockin' me out."

A gasp falls from my lips as shock radiates through me like a wave crashing onto the shore.

"What? Oh my God."

Sully nods, then shrugs. "Aye, it feckin' hurt. When I woke up and opened my eyes, Ma was lyin' on the floor beside me—her nose broken, blood drippin' from her face, and a cut under her left eye that had swollen to the point she couldn't see out of it."

Tears well in my eyes, and I reach for his hand. He allows me to take it, and I hold on to Sully like he's a lifeline, and I hope I can be one for him. I can't imagine watching your mother go through that. But then I experienced much the same kind of abuse, only I didn't have kids to witness it.

"I vowed ta kill the fecker," Sully continues. "The next day, I woke up with a new plan in mind. I was goin'ta get the bastard back fer what he did. He still kept comin' round the house. He would either coax Ma into takin' him back, or he'd be fightin' with her. It got worse and worse."

"Oh, Sully," I lean in and bring his hand to my lips. I want to hold him, but I wait until he makes the move. "I'm so sorry you had to go through that, and I'm sorry your mother had to live with such a vile monster."

"It took me a few years, and by the time I was fourteen, I had built muscle. I was stronger. I was in the boxin' club every feckin' day. I wanted ta be able ta take on the bastard and win."

He looks at me then, and I see it in his eyes. There's a clarity shimmering there. He's proud of himself, and I am too. I didn't think I could ever feel like that.

Be proud of a man who killed another, but I am. I'm thankful he took it into his own hands because, more times than not, it could have ended a completely different way.

Sully swigs his beer, and I can tell he's nervous. I know something happened. I recall he told me back when we first met at the centre. The ghosts of the past haunt him. It's so clear to see on his face. His expression is dark, filled with anger.

"One night, I came home, and he was there," Sully continues his story. "There was nothing to stop me because I'd grown up. I'd made sure I could fight him before I confronted him again. There comes a point in life when you need to make a choice. When you need ta make sure there's nothin' you'll regret."

"True, but decisions can change as well," I say to him as I consider my own secrets, my past.

"Aye, they can, but with him, I knew I would never stop until he was out of Ma's life. And even then, I didn't think he would just walk out. He needed to be forced out."

Forced. Killed.

The words linger in my mind, hanging there like a lead weight. I'm now even more sure about what Sully did.

When he looks at me again, there's no regret or guilt

in his eyes. His expression remains neutral, and I know I'm going to see the true nature of this man. He may think it's bad, and I shouldn't be here with him, but I'm not afraid. I'm not at all scared, because I know who he is. He's a good man.

"I took the fecker out of Ma's house that night. I dragged him outside, and I took him to a park that sat behind the houses where we lived."

"Were you alone?" I can't imagine a young Sully, even if he had been working out, taking on a grown man. But when he nods, my mouth falls open.

"Feckin' adrenaline had kicked in, and I didn't feel anythin' but the rage I'd been holding' back all those years. Ma ran after me, but I told her ta stay inside. There wasn't any reason fer her to see me like that. I was nothin' more than a beast, ragin' at the bastard I'd finally captured."

Sully's voice gets quieter as he speaks, and with every decibel it lowers, a shiver races down my spine. Knowing he's killed with his bare hands has my stomach twisting, but I know he did it for a good reason. He was protecting the woman who loves him and who he loves. And no matter what he says to me, I know I'll never see him as a monster. He's a hero.

"Not all heroes wear shiny armor," I tell him with a

small smile, and it causes him to chuckle.

"Ach, aye, but I took a life that day. I stole it, and I knew there was no goin' back." He leans back into the sofa, and I wait for him to tell me the rest. "I took a knife ta him before I strangled him. And I didn't blink. There were no second guesses, and I didn't want to stop. I needed him out of my ma's life, and I believed it was the only way."

I want to tell him I believe that, too. Because I'm pretty sure his mother would have kept taking Conall back, even after all he'd done to her. That's the problem with loving someone like that. It always ends in pain, and no matter how many times they apologize, there's nothing that will change them. Darkness will always take over, and it will be there until you're the one in the hospital. Which is what happened to me. I only accepted I needed to run when I almost died.

Even then, it wasn't like I could easily escape. Rogan would have found me no matter where I went if I'd stayed in the US. It may be a big country, but there are eyes watching everywhere. I'm the daughter of a dead MC President, and too many people know me.

I suffered in silence for too long because I didn't believe there was a way out. Not until the opportunity came while I was in that hospital bed. When the nurse walked in and told me she could release me early, I realized this was my chance. The nurse knew about my abuse—everyone in that hospital knew the moment I came in. There were old scars, fading bruises, and there were fractures from past nights of Rogan being angry. I couldn't hide the damage any longer.

"I didn't regret it then, and I don't now." Sully's voice drags me back to the present.

"I didn't think you would, and you shouldn't," I tell him earnestly. "Your mother needed you and you were there for her. You should be proud that you could save her from a worse fate."

Sully looks at me once more and takes my hand. "What I need ye ta know is I enjoyed killing him. I reveled in it, and I know I shouldn't have. What kinda man does that make me?"

"It makes you someone who'd do anything to protect those you love," I say. It's what I believe, and nothing he tells me will change my mind. "You may not see it that way just yet, but it's true."

He shakes his head, and I know he's going to try to argue with me. But I'm not listening to him. I don't want to, because I know he's a good person. There's no denying it. Ever.

"Listen to me," I say as I scoot closer to him. "You're a

man who'll do anything in your power to keep innocent people safe. It doesn't matter if you know them or not. Even when we met at the rehab centre, I could see you for who you truly are. I've always been afraid around men. It's just part of who I am. But with you..."

Sully watches me as I try to find the words to describe what I'm thinking. I'm not sure anymore. I just need him to know I'm here, and I'm not leaving him.

Finally, I continue, "...With you, I feel safe. I know you won't hurt me, and I know that no matter what happens between us, I'll always care about you."

In some ways, I'm trying to tell him I've fucked up, and I don't want him to hate me. But, instead of telling him the truth, I lean in and press my lips to his.

My chest tightens when he pulls me close and wraps his arms around me, holding me against him. Sully's body is beautiful. Every dip and peak of his chest, torso, and arms are like granite.

"Thank ye fer listenin' ta me," Sully murmurs against my lips.

I know what's coming next, and I want to delay it for as long as I possibly can. But the man before me, the one holding onto me, is far too intelligent to fall for my games. And I realize it's time for me to give him a bit more insight into my past.

"Ye know what I want. Don't ye?" he asks.

I nod and blink back the tears that are fighting to escape. They'll fall. I know they will, and the moment I start crying, I don't know if I'm ever going to be able to stop. The fear of scaring Sully away runs rife through my veins.

"Hey," he says as he cups my face in his powerful hands. "I'm not goin' anywhere. Ye will tell me what ye can, and we'll work through it together."

Perhaps it's the fact I'm accepting him for who he is that makes him believe I'm a good person. I used to be, but then I broke, and I lost all the goodness inside me.

And now, I'm lying to a man I'm falling hard for.

CHAPTER 8

Clover

It's time for me to finally tell him everything. Well, everything about my past with Rogan, which I've tried so hard to hide from. But there's no longer a reason to keep it secret. Sully has an inkling of what I've been through, and now he's going to hear the rest of the story.

It's difficult for me to think about. Sully doesn't move. I'm not even sure he's breathing when I look up at him. There's affection in his dark eyes, and I offer a small, shy smile before I take a deep breath and start to speak.

"When I was eighteen, I thought I knew everything." I can't stop the small smile on my lips. There were many times my dad's best friend, Darius, told me to be careful. "Darius wanted me to go to art school, and I did for a while. He took over the club after Dad died, and I allowed him to be there for me. As a surrogate father."

"I remember meetin' him," Sully says then. "He was ye da's right-hand man fer years. I didn't spend too long with him, but I recall yer da spoke highly of him."

I nod. "Yeah, he stood by Dad through a lot of shit that went down at the club. They were like brothers. And then, when I met Rogan, I thought life was going to change for the better. My sadness at losing Dad had eased up by then, and everything seemed to be improving. I was convinced I was in love, and that Rogan was good."

"And there were no signs in the beginning," Sully says with a slow nod of his head.

He must remember what his mother's boyfriend was like. Men like Rogan and Conall don't show their true colors until after you're in too deep. Because if they do it too early, there's still time to run.

I sit back, crossing my legs on the sofa while facing

Sully. Before I continue, I finish my water and set the glass down on the floor.

It's time to get real. "I moved in with him while I was studying. Things were going so well between us I thought there was no point in waiting. I didn't want to delay what I believed was inevitable. I wanted a ring, a white picket fence, the whole lot."

Sully sits quietly. I'm not sure how he feels about hearing that, but I need to be honest about what I was going through. My dreams about a happy ever after were always at the forefront of my mind. And Rogan was nice to me. He was attentive and caring.

"I thought I'd found a good man," I continue. "He didn't scream or shout. He didn't even fight with me. There were no arguments in the beginning."

"And ye fell in love," Sully says then. "It's understandable. When someone treats ye right, there's no stoppin' the heart from what it wants." He takes my hand, but doesn't make another move to pull me closer. And I'm thankful because I need the space to continue. I know if Sully took me in his arms right now, I couldn't continue my story.

"I wanted to believe things were great, but looking back, I realize there were small signs. He would buy my clothes and tell me what looked *good* on me. When I was out with friends, he would message and call constantly, asking where I was. At the start, I truly believed it was innocent concern."

When I recall all those moments I thought he was being a loving boyfriend, I can now see how he was trying to control every aspect of my life.

"I'd given up studying, not long after I moved in with him, but then I landed an internship at a local company. I was going to learn about art and curation, a deviation from my dream of a tattoo parlor, but it would have paid more. I was earning a good salary, and I was finally at ease with everything. Darius was running the club, so I didn't need to go back and be the princess everyone expected me to be. It wasn't something I could have faced."

"And that's when he turned?" Sully stares at me. The concern on his face is palpable. With those dark eyes boring into me, I know I need to dive in now, headfirst.

I nod. "Yeah, he didn't like that I was working, that I had male co-workers. Nothing made him happy. I would get home from work and make dinner. I would do anything he wanted. And then one night, after a late evening at work, I came home to him smashing every plate and cup we had. I wasn't sure what happened, but the moment I walked into the apartment, he was on me. His hand around my throat—"

I stop for a moment, needing to breathe. The memory floods my mind, and there's nothing I can do but lose myself to it. The pain of his fingers is still so real, it's as if he's here, holding me against the wall.

"I'm here," Sully soothes with a gentle squeeze of my hand. "Open yer eyes. Look at me." His words sink deep into my chest, and I force my lashes to flutter open.

"He pinned me against the wall," I choke out as I remember. "He was in my face, anger raging through him like an inferno."

I can tell from the way Sully's eyes flick left and right that he's trying to tamp down his own anger. But it's not directed at me. He's livid at what Rogan did to me.

"I tried to explain that I'd been working late, but he didn't hear me. It was as if he was possessed. Like an entity had taken over his body. He choked me until I was almost passing out, and then he threw me to the ground. And..."

I look away before I push to my feet and head to the window. The floor to ceiling view of Belfast sits before me as I stare out at the twinkling lights. The tears I've been fighting escape, and they trickle down my cheeks.

"We don't have ta do this," Sully says from behind

me, as he wraps his arms around me.

"It was the first time," I whisper, my voice hoarse as I speak. "His boot... he..." The memory is so fresh in my mind. I recall the agony of my ribs being fractured. I can still see the blue and purple bruises all over my fair skin. "It was the first time I ended up in the hospital."

"And he apologized when he realized what he'd done," Sully finishes for me.

All I can do is nod. It was the first time I ended up in the ER, but it wasn't the last.

"There were other times when his abuse was less serious, but still painful. He took..." I swallow back the lump in my throat as I look at Sully's reflection in the window. "He took a lighter, a Zippo, and heated the lid of the lighter with the flame before he pressed it against the inside of my upper arm. He only did it because I made a joke about him not needing another drink while we were in the pub."

Sully's fingers tighten on my shoulders. It's not painful—it's as if he's trying to hold me up but also keep himself from breaking something. There's a calm surety that he's with me and I'm with him.

"One day he found me in the bathroom with a blade," I whisper as the tears stream down my cheeks. I don't wipe them away, because I want to feel them.

I need to expel them from my body. There was a time I didn't cry, even when he hurt me. I realized quickly that he wanted me to shed tears. He enjoyed it, so I became an emotionless doll.

"Ye don't have ta—"

"He took the blade from my hands, and he cut my arms. From my elbow down to my wrist. He laughed when he looked at me and said I was worthless."

I shake my head when I remember how Rogan smirked as he watched me bleed. Above the sadness and heartbreak currently racing through me, I feel my anger at him, at myself for staying, even after that.

"He rushed me to the hospital. The story was that I was depressed and tried to kill myself. He was the doting boyfriend, worried about me."

"I can't lie to ye," Sully says as he rests his chin on my shoulder. "I'm livid right now. And there's no doubt I could so easily kill him at this very second."

There's a stark contrast between the affectionate way he's holding me and the words he's speaking. And it makes me want to smile that he's so protective of me. I've never had someone like that. Well, not after Dad. Even though I had Darius, there was still a distance between us. I'm sure he and the rest of the brothers would kill for me, but there's something different about this because it's Sully. He's the man who's slowly stolen my heart and is holding it in his hands.

I turn in his arms and look up at him. There are so many emotions dancing in his eyes at this moment, but the one I see the most is love.

"I don't want anyone hurtin' ye ever again, even me," he says to me, which makes my heart thud wildly against my ribs. "No woman should have ta go through what ye did, and it makes me angry to know there are men out there who do this to beautiful, innocent women."

"You're a good man, Sully. That's why I told you, no matter what is in your past, you're nothing like Rogan or the others who think it's okay to take their hurt out on someone else."

"Why did ye stay with him fer so long?"

It's the age-old question. It's the one thing I ask myself, and I'm pretty sure other women in that position ask themselves all the time. I remember watching movies way back, and I wondered why the hell women didn't get out of those kinds of relationships. It plagued me, but then, when I was in one, I learned how easy it is to get stuck in the loop of abuse, apologies, and forgiveness.

"It's not as easy as just walking away. There's fear,

there's emotion, and even though there is pain, I also felt love. When you care that much about someone, you want to believe them when they say they're sorry."

I'm not sure that's the answer he wants, but it's the only one I have. I hoped and prayed, but in the end, I could never change Rogan. Accepting he was nothing more than a monster was crushing because I wanted to believe he was good for so long.

"I guess in some ways, I thought if I loved him harder, if I showed him I'm not running away, then he'd become a better man. And as I say that now, I realize how stupid it sounds."

Sully shakes his head. "No, not stupid. Ye just sound like ye're capable of seein' good in people. There's nothin' wrong with that, but there are times ye need to recognize that not everyone has good in them."

His hand trails down my side as those dark eyes pierce me. The gentle way Sully touches me calms all the fears I've lived with when it comes to men.

He pulls me into his arms and leans in to press his lips to mine. All the hurt and pain diminishes, and when I feel his tongue probing for entrance, I allow it. I want it more than anything. His hands grip my butt, and he pulls me even closer. Sully lifts me against him, and my legs wrap around his waist. I'm not going anywhere, and neither is he.

He carries me to the bedroom where he lowers me onto the mattress and hovers above me. His hair falls on either side of his face, and I tangle my fingers in the locks of brown.

There's a frantic need coursing through us both as I tug at his top, and he discards the material to the floor. His chest is pure perfection as he kneels up and helps me out of my clothes.

"Tonight, ye're in charge," he tells me with a salacious grin, and he lies back on the bed, allowing me to tug his jeans off.

I ease out of my underwear, and the way Sully's fiery gaze trails over me makes me shiver with desire.

I crawl up between his thick, spread thighs and then tease his erection with my fingers. The hardness throbs in my hand as I grip him and slowly stroke him over the material of his boxers. A deep rumble vibrates in his chest as he looks down at me. Desire flickers in his stare, and I can't help but smile.

When I finally tug his underwear down, his cock is hard and rigid. And I allow my tongue to swirl over the tip, the flavor of him bursting on my tongue when I lick him from the base to the head where there's a silver piercing that I know feels incredible when he's inside me.

"Feck," Sully growls when I wrap my lips around him, and I savor him like a hungry kitten. He tastes like heaven and hell, all in one package. It isn't long before he pulls me off and says, "If ye keep that up, I'll come before I'm inside ye, and that's where I want to be right now."

I don't need any more coaxing. I quickly straddle his hips and ease myself down onto his hard shaft. With every inch of him that enters, I whimper as he stretches me. Sully's hands are on my hips, and he holds me steady until he's all the way inside me. It's a fullness I've never felt before, not until we took this intimate step all those months ago.

I don't want anyone else inside me, and I'm beyond turned on, dripping over him as I ride his cock.

"Ye look like a feckin' angel, wee lass," he tells me as he watches me move. "Feckin' saintly," he growls when I lean over him, my nipples pressed against his chest. Every hard part of him molds to the softness of me.

We move in sync. It's as if we're two parts of a whole, and we've finally found each other. The brokenness of me and the shattered shards of him fit together perfectly. I didn't think it was possible to feel so much love, so much emotion.

"Clover," Sully groans as he holds me steady so I can't move. "Feck." And then he lifts his hips to fuck me.

There's no holding back. He leans his head forward to capture my nipple in his mouth. His teeth graze the peak, and he bites down, causing me to convulse and shiver. I'm so close to the edge, and I know he is, too.

He thrusts deep inside me, so fucking deep I nearly scream when he rubs against the part of me that has stars sparking behind my eyelids. There's no going back, and I don't want to. I'm forever his, and he is mine. Now all we need is to break down the last few walls.

Sully's cock thickens, and he reaches between us to pinch my clit as his cock massages my inner walls and he sends me over the edge. My body locks on top of his, and I feel him lose control. His cock pulses, and he fills me with his release as I soak him in mine.

We lie there for a long while in the darkness and the silence. It's a beautiful moment. We shed our demons, and they danced together in bliss.

But, I know that when tomorrow comes, there's still so much more to figure out.

CHAPTER 9

There were so many things about me I didn't want Clover ta know. So many things she should never be privy to. And yet, when I wake beside her, I realise I've told her those things now and she's still here. The things that burned my tongue when I thought of confessin' them to her are now out in the open.

When you love someone, you can't hide anythin' from them. I've learned that watchin' Monster and Miren and seein' how Tye is with his girl. I want that closeness with Clover, but I know that even though she admitted a lot ta me last night, there's still things she's hidin'. The secrets dance in her eyes, and each time I look at her, I realise there's much more ta the wee lass than meets the eye.

I leave her to sleep and head into the kitchen. I haven't warned her about McCallum yet, but this morning will be time fer that. She needs to keep an eye open because if he knows about her, there's no doubt he would use her against me. That's the problem about this life. When yer enemies know ye have a weakness, they'll jump on the chance ta blackmail ye with shite.

It's why I've spent most of my life alone. There are things I never want to go through, and that includes losin' someone I love. And I know fer a fact, I'm in love with Clover. She's the one good thing in my life besides my brothers.

With my focus on the coffee machine, I flick it on and wait for the water to heat. Slowly, the liquid drips into the mug I've placed below it.

"You're up early," Clover says from behind me, and I set the mug of fresh coffee down in front of her. "Thank you."

"I couldn't sleep," I tell her. "Needed to get some caffeine down before I tell ye about the men who are behind the blackmail I mentioned last night."

"What men?" She leans her hip against the counter.

Grabbing my mug, I head into the living room, and she follows. We settle on the sofa, and I swallow a mouthful of coffee.

"The night I killed Ma's boyfriend," I start the story. "There was a man who saw me. He's not a good person, but at the time, I thought I needed help covering up my crime."

"He took advantage of your innocence," Clover says, and I nod. "And now he has something he's holding over you."

"Aye," I say to her, thinking about what I have ta do. There's no doubt I'm goin'ta do what McCallum wants. And the arsehole won't stop houndin' me until I do. "I need ye to be careful when ye're in the bar. He doesn't know about ye yet, but I have no doubt he'll find out. The man has a lot of resources."

"I understand, and I will be careful, but you need to watch your back as well. I can't live with the idea of something happening to you because..." Her words filter off into silence, and I know what she wants ta say. It's written all over her face, but she doesn't admit the words I realise I want ta hear.

"I'm not goin' anywhere," I tell Clover as I look at

her.

The fear in her eyes makes my chest tighten. I'm fallin' fer her, and I can't fight it anymore. But even so, I'm not lettin' my heart go before she tells me what she's hidin'. I'll have ta wait it out, and fer her, I'll do it.

"I know you're not. I'm just worried because I finally have something worth losing. I don't know if I can survive if you leave me." Clover's eyes fill with tears, and I take her hand before scootin' closer to her.

"I'm not goin' anywhere," I repeat, keepin' her stare hostage as I say it because I don't want her to think I'm jokin'.

Even if she has secrets, I want her to know I'm here. There's no runnin' anymore. It's new to me, but I can stay just fer her.

"And neither am I," she tells me with a small smile on her lips. "Nobody is going to take me away from you. They may try, but they won't succeed."

"I'm goin'ta find that bastard who hurt you," I tell her, reminding her just what my plans are. There's no way I'm walkin' away from what I want ta do. Clover's expression changes from affectionate to afraid. The furrow between her brows deepens. "He needs ta pay," I say with all the confidence in the feckin' world.

"I know you're angry, and you hate him, but I don't

know if I'm ready to face Rogan. There are so many things he did to me, things I don't want to think about ever again. I don't know if I'm going to be able to look him in the eye."

"I get ye," I respond with a nod. "But ye also can't live a life where ye're constantly afraid he's goin'ta come after ye."

I know what it's like walkin' around while havin'ta keep lookin' over yer shoulder. It's not a life to live.

"If he wanted to find me," she says slowly. "He would have done so by now. I don't think he's even bothered I'm gone. Perhaps he's moved on."

"Moved on ta another innocent woman?" I challenge.

The thought of that feckin' arsehole hurtin' other women makes my blood boil even more. I never once considered I'd have to kill fer the same reason I did in the past. I thought that was a one-off fer me, but I'll gladly do it again if it'll keep Clover safe. The woman before me already means so much more ta me than I ever expected.

"There are women out there livin' in fear," I tell her. "And if I can eliminate at least one more of those feckers who instil that fear, I'll do it."

Clover looks at me, and her expression softens. A small smile dances on her lips as she regards me. I know there are no guarantees that this will work between us, but I want her safe. That's all. Her da was a good friend ta me, and if I can make sure his little girl lives a happy life, I'll do it. Even if it means one day, she moves on from this place and me.

"Then I'll support your plan," Clover says. "I don't want anyone going through what I did. I can't bear the thought of it. There's something else I was thinking about as well."

"Aye?"

Clover nods. "I want to go to therapy, to talk to someone about my past. I think facing my past and talking about it could help me. I also want to volunteer at the local women's centre."

I know the one she means. It's the one where Ma used to work. She would go in there every day and make sure there were enough supplies for those who were runnin' from abusive homes. The centre was set up a long time ago, and those working there see an influx of women comin' through its doors on a weekly basis.

"I like the idea of that," I tell her. "If ye think ye're ready ta talk ta someone, then do it. I can't say I believe in all that shite, but I know it helped Ma."

Clover grins. "You believe that killing someone will

help? That's your coping strategy. But for me, talking will help me work through all the memories that still haunt me."

This time, I pull her closer and press my lips ta hers. The idea of her healin' from her pain makes me happy.

"I'll support ye with whatever ye want ta do." It's a promise I make her, one I'll never break because she's special ta me. I want her to be whole again. "I may not be the only one who can help put yer pieces back together, but I will feckin' try my hardest to make sure ye're happy again."

Clover looks at me as she smiles, the corners of her mouth tiltin' upwards, her eyes sparklin'.

"I am happy, Sully. You've brought so much warmth into my life. You've given me the safety I haven't had in such a long time. Since Dad was alive. I didn't think I would ever feel like this again."

As much as I want to hear her say the three little words that would make me run a mile, she doesn't. But then again, I'm not sure I would run, not with her. I never expected to love someone, never in my lifetime. I've seen far too much shite ta want that pure, passionate emotion that so many people would kill fer.

"Well, I can try to make ye feel that fer as long as ye'll have me. I don't expect ye ta stick around forever, but I'll always look after ye."

This makes her frown. "Why wouldn't I stick around forever?"

Her question stills me fer a wee while. I don't know why, but there's this twist in my gut when I consider her walkin' away. Perhaps it's because I know she's still hidin' somethin' from me. My gut feelin' has never been wrong. But I don't tell her that.

"All I'm sayin' is that if ever ye feel the need to move on," I respond with a little white lie instead. "If there is somethin' ye want ta do with yer life, then ye do it." I'm not sure I'm makin' any sense, but the idea of forever, of puttin' a ring on her finger, scares the shite out of me.

There are too many variables fer us ta get past right now. When I find Rogan, all hell could break loose and then we're goin'ta have ta work through it. Then there's Bragan, and there's McCallum. The threats ta both our lives could change things so easily. The future is never certain.

"I get that," Clover whispers. "But I don't want to leave. It's not even crossed my mind to consider walking out of here. I don't want to leave Belfast."

"Ye still have yer da's club that's rightfully yours," I tell her.

She's still a club princess. This girl could run her own motorcycle club. It's an honour to say the least. Fer her to turn her back on her family, it's not a good sign to the rest of the brothers.

"I know." She sighs as she looks away from me. "I just never wanted to live that life without Dad. You understand?"

I do understand where she's comin' from, so I nod. "Aye, I get ye." It can't be easy livin' with the memory of losin' a parent ye love so much. It's an everyday reminder they're no longer with ye. "But ye have ta remember, if ye do decide to run the club, he'll be proud of ye. And if ye decide ta do somethin' else, he'll still be lookin' down on ye with love and pride."

This makes her smile, and I see the tears wellin' up in her eyes. She's a strong woman, fightin' back emotion. Over the past months, there've been moments when I've noticed she gets lost in her head. God knows I do the same, time and time again.

Memories are feckin' horrible things that seem to slam into ye when ye least expect them. But I believe they're there to remind us we're still alive. They also confirm that our lives are real, and we're not just walkin' around like zombies. We have experiences that shape us, and if I had ta be honest, I wouldn't change a thing. Even the most difficult times of my life.

I cup Clover's face in my hands and hold her steady so she can't look away from me. I lock my gaze with hers because I want her ta listen, to take in what I am about ta say.

"Whatever yer life brings ye, good and bad, it's made ye a beautiful, strong woman. And I don't want ye to fight those emotions. If ye need ta cry, my shoulder is big enough to handle that. And if ye want ta laugh, do it, because I feckin' love the sound."

We stare at each other fer a wee while. Lookin' into her eyes makes my heart slam against my ribs. It's a wild, thrummin' rhythm I can't deny. But I won't admit what I'm feelin' fer her, not just yet.

I'm about to speak when my phone buzzes in my pocket, and I sigh because I know it's Monster. The fecker has the timin' of a cock block.

I release Clover and pull the device out, but I find it's Tye instead.

"What's up, mate?" I respond by way of greetin'.

"I have somethin' fer ye," he tells me, and my gut churns with excitement and anger.

"Ye've found the bastard?" I ask, but I know the answer already. He doesn't need to confirm it, because that's the only reason he'd be callin' me.

"Aye, he actually got on a flight last night," Tye tells me, and I can practically hear the smile on his face. Wee fecker is always proud when he's got into a job and cracked it.

"He's comin' here," I say with the realisation that the man who hurt Clover will soon be on the same soil as me.

"Aye," Tye finally says, which affirms what I've been thinkin'.

There's no longer any doubt in my mind. I'm goin'ta get the revenge I need, and so is Clover.

"I'll be there soon. Tell Monster I'm goin'ta need help." I hang up before Tye can say anythin' more. I look at Clover, who's watchin' me intently. "Rogan is on his way to Belfast."

"What?" Panic sets in when she realises she's goin'ta have ta face the bastard sooner than she expected.

"He'll probably be landin' this afternoon. If you want ta go ta work, I'll have Tye and a few of the prospects watchin' the pub. I'm not goin'ta leave ye alone, but I am goin'ta get the arsehole the moment he lands."

"Sully—"

"And then I'm takin' him ta the warehouse where I'll make sure he's ready fer ye," I tell her. "Will ye be ready if I call on ye ta come?"

She looks as if she's seen a ghost. She would never have been able to hide forever, though. There's no way. Men like him—they never move on. They come back, repeatedly, and this time, he's comin' fer her.

Then she nods. "I'll be ready. But please don't do anything stupid." The plea in her tone is obvious.

"I won't," I say before I pause fer a moment. "But I can't promise, if the bastard provokes me, I won't make him bleed."

And I already know I'll have more blood on my hands today. She may not want me ta commit another murder, but I'll gladly do it fer her. It feels as if I've come full circle. There's no goin' back now.

CHAPTER 10

I didn't tell him the truth. I should have, but I realized that if Sully ever found out about my family, the part he has no clue about, he'd hate me forever. The truth's been kept under wraps, and for now, I'm safe, but I've a feeling that won't last much longer.

There are so many things I haven't been able to confess to Sully. If he knew, he would lose his mind. I'm only just getting to know him properly, and I don't want him to go on a rampage for me.

I don't need a hero.

I'm strong enough to protect myself. But somehow, deep down, I know he won't listen to me and still defend me in any way he can.

I'm wiping down the bar when the door swings open, and my stomach drops as three men in suits walk in. I didn't expect them because they shouldn't be here. But I know who sent them, so there's no use in hiding anything from these men. They're experts in their line of work, and if I try to do anything untoward, they'll kill me.

Many times over the years, I've been close to death. I've had to survive somehow. There wasn't any other choice. If I'd given up too easily, I wouldn't be around right now. Fighting is in my DNA.

"What can I do for you?" I ask the three men who have now found a permanent space by the bar.

I can't deny I'm scared. My heart is thudding against my chest painfully, a reminder that I'm never truly safe. It doesn't matter what country I live in, there'll always be people out to get me.

"Yer uncle wanted us to check in on ye," one of them says. He appears to be the one in charge and the spokesperson for the trio. He's in a dark suit and looks like he could easily crush me with one hand. "We have a problem. He doesn't like the company ye're keepin'."

"He doesn't have a say in shit," I tell them, realizing I'm running my mouth, and they could kill me. "I mean, I'm doing what he wants. He wants the pub to run properly, and I'm doing that. I've had no issues, so I don't see what the problem is. My friends are my business."

Even as I say it, I realize I could end up dead behind the bar. If I did, I know Sully would find me, and he'd seek revenge. But then again, he's already after the man in question.

"Stop hangin' out with the Royal Bastards. The biker with the long hair will be taken care of if you can't control yerself," the one in charge tells me. There's no room for debate in his voice, and I realize not only am I being watched, they're watching Sully too.

His words cause mine to fail. I don't know what to tell them. I can't stand the thought of never seeing Sully again, but I don't want to put him in any danger. I'm at a fucking crossroads, and I need to make a choice.

If I went to Sully and told him the truth, he could one of two things. He could hate me and tell me to leave. Or, he could tell me it doesn't matter and not to put myself in danger. That would mean he would probably lock me up and never allow me to see the light of day again. Not until he's dealt with these oafs.

"Stay away from the club," the one in charge demands once more.

There's an underlying threat he's not voicing, and I don't want to find out what he'd do to me if I refuse his request, so I nod.

"Fine." The lie tastes like a poison on my tongue—a toxin that will slowly kill me. And I don't know how to stop it eating away at my body.

There's a stare down between us. One I don't want, but I can't avoid. He studies me with a shrewd gaze for a moment before nodding in finality, and the three men leave the pub.

If they're watching me, I cannot be seen at the club, and I definitely can't be with Sully. The thought causes my chest to tighten with panic. It's only been a short time, but I can't imagine my life without him. And now I'm going to have to say goodbye. I can't allow him to get into a fight with my uncle. He's dangerous, I know he is, and if I put Sully at any risk, I'll never forgive myself.

Perhaps it's easier if I leave. I can pack my bags and take my chances back at the Kovenant. They're my people, and I know they'll keep me safe. Also, when Rogan arrives here, he'll learn I'm gone, and he'll have no reason to stay in Belfast. It will be easier to do it that way.

Thankfully, the prospects Sully is sending haven't arrived yet. If they had, they'd have seen the men walking in here and that would have kicked off a war I'm not prepared for.

Heading to White Pass, back to my childhood home, will be better for everyone. Even though I told Sully I won't leave him, I know there's no way I can ignore the fact my life is putting those I care about in life-threatening danger.

When the door swings open again, I expect to see the Royal Bastards' prospects walking in, but instead I see a face from my past. A man I never wanted to see again.

The smirk on his face tells me there's nothing I can do to escape him. Now he's found me, he's going to make sure I never run from him again.

"What are you doing here?" I bite out.

Anger, fear, and concern trickle through me. It's a subtle movement, but I see him pull a knife from his pocket, and I step back instinctively. I know the weapon—I've seen it before. Rogan flicks the lock of the door, and I'm now shut in the pub alone with a man who's going to kill me. I have no doubt in my mind that's why he's come here.

"I was worried about my little slut," he tells me, his voice taking on an almost demonic tone. Rage burns in his eyes with every step he takes toward me. "I hear you're now fucking a biker," he says as he nears the bar. "I mean, I always figured you'd want to do that after you lost your biker daddy all those years ago. Is that why I wasn't good enough for you?"

"Rogan, please, you don't have to do this. We can walk away from this. We're both moving on, and we can—"

"Like fuck am I moving on," he shouts, causing me to jump in surprise.

My hands are shaking so much I can't hold on to the cloth I've been holding, and it drops to the floor. If I can get to my phone, perhaps I can call Sully without Rogan noticing.

Sully said they'd be looking for Rogan at the airport, but it looks like he's outsmarted them. Surely, they'll figure out this was the first place he'd come. Sully will know. He'll be here soon.

"You think you can just walk away from what we had?" Rogan says as he pulls a chair out from one of the tables. He swings it around and straddles the seat the wrong way. Those dark, almost demonic eyes pin me to the spot as he watches me. He rests his forearms on the back of the chair and leans forward.

"I just need you to leave. I'm happy here, and you can move on." The suggestion makes him chuckle, but it's not amusement I hear in the sound, it's derision.

He shakes his head slowly as he regards me. "I was under the impression your little cunt loved when I used it."

"Rogan," I plead, hoping he'll see how desperate I am to just leave, and how I want him to go. But that's the one thing I learned about Rogan over the years—when he's in this kind of mood, there's no talking to him. No matter how hard I try, he'll never respect my needs. "If you leave now—"

"If I leave now, I won't be able to show you how much I missed you," he tells me as he pushes to his feet.

I'm stuck behind the counter. There's only one way out, and it's at the far end of the bar where Rogan's now blocking the exit.

"The pub is opening soon," I don't know if the warning will anger him or if it will make sure he thinks twice about what he's doing, but for a moment, I see a flicker of hesitation in his eyes. But almost as soon as it appears, it's gone, and I'm left staring at the face of my tormentor.

He takes slow, deliberate steps toward me, and I know there's nothing I can do but wait it out. If I can calm him down, I can stall him until I find a way to escape.

"Let me pour you a drink. We can talk." I pray with all I have that the offer calms him, but he doesn't stop his steps.

He nears me until his body is flush against mine. I have to tip my head back to look at him, and in those dark eyes, I see the anger and rage spilling over. It's like lava exploding from a volcano. I don't know how long we stand in silence before Rogan lifts the blade.

"It's been far too long since I've seen you. I've waited months for this," he tells me with a smirk curling his lips.

I still can't believe I spent so long with a man like this. I saw the best in him, or I tried to, but now, looking into his stare, I realize there's no good anywhere in him. He made a fool of me, and I was stupid enough to believe his lies. The pain that radiates through me when the metal slithers over the sensitive skin of my cheek causes me to whimper.

"You always looked so much prettier when you cried," Rogan hisses into my face as he leans in. His tongue darts out, and he licks at the wound he's inflicted. I cower at the motion, at feeling his saliva on my flesh. "It made my dick so hard when you used to beg. It was a beautiful thing seeing you fear me."

"You made sure I wanted no one else ever again," I tell him earnestly.

There were times over the months, over the years, I believed that maybe my life didn't come with a happy ending. Mine, more than likely, would come when Rogan finally got what he wanted—me dead.

"I bet that big, bad biker you're hanging around with will say you're a good fuck," Rogan says, his lip curling in disgust as he looks at me. "I bet you've swallowed his dick already. Spread your legs for him just like the whore I know you are."

"You believe what you need to," I tell him.

I shouldn't be goading the predator, but I can't help myself. I want to see if he'll take the bait. If he'll finally admit to wanting me dead. All the time I was with him, I was certain that one day I wouldn't wake up from one of his attacks. I guessed he would tell people I took my own life. I even thought about doing it, time and again, but something always stopped me.

Perhaps it was my father's words to *never give up*, to *fight until your last breath*. But I do understand why people feel compelled to end it all. There have been many times I pondered leaping over the edge while knowing I won't be hurt ever again.

Deep down, though, I just wasn't brave enough because I knew the toll it would have on those I left behind. I didn't have Dad anymore, but I still had the brothers of the MC, and I knew my death would burden them because they couldn't save me.

The brothers care about me, even though I was the one who walked out on the club when they asked me to step into my father's shoes. At the time, I was more focused on my needs. I wanted to be with Rogan. I didn't think of the future beyond where I was. But now I've learned my lesson, and I'm saddened that I allowed those thoughts of having a *normal* life, away from the Kovenant MC, to take over. All I ever wanted was to be happy.

Losing both my parents culminated in me losing myself. It's the worst thing I could have done, but it happened.

I look at Rogan and say, "I just want to be free."

That's all I feel the need to tell him, and as I utter the last word, I step into the knife and allow the blade to pierce through my clothing into the flesh of my right hip. But as I do, there's a loud ringing in my ears, and Rogan goes down beside me, causing me to slump back onto the counter.

On the other side of the bar, dressed in a navy blue suit, is a man I've only seen glimpses of in the past, but I know exactly who he is. He comes to me quickly and pulls the blade from my left hip. It didn't go deep enough to be fatal, thankfully.

"Ye're gettin' yerself into trouble, wee Clover. Luckily, ye uncle Patrick is here ta save ye," Patrick Bragan says with a smile.

Bragan, the name that has been synonymous with violence and danger all my life. He was Dad's elder brother, well, half-brother. Same mother, different fathers. When my dad was still a young boy, his father moved him away from Ireland, leaving Patrick to take over the mob. At least, that's what I learned when I was growing up.

"Aren't ye goin'ta thank me fer what I've just done, wee Clover?"

I don't know the rest of the story, and I don't want to know, considering this is the man the Royal Bastards are after. I recall the night I overheard them talking about him. He's done some horrific things. And he's not someone I want to have in my life.

"Thank you for saving me. But I have a feeling you'll want something from me for doing it," I say.

He may be family, but I don't know him. He's a stranger to me. But if Sully walked in here now, he wouldn't believe I don't know Patrick. After all, why would the head of the Irish mob save me? I'm a nobody.

"You should leave," I tell him.

"Should I?" He tips his head to the side. "Because ye're wee boyfriend is comin'ta save ye?" There's a challenge in his eyes, and I know this man will gladly stay here and throw me under the bus. "I wonder what he'd do if he were ta find out that ye're my niece."

I don't know what to say. There's no response that will make this okay. Even if my uncle left now, I couldn't explain the dead body beside the bar with a bullet wound to his chest. I don't own a gun, and the gunshot that killed Rogan is obvious. If Sully walked in here now, I'd have to tell him the truth, and I know he'd want nothing more to do with me.

"I want ye to give Sully a message from me," Patrick says. "Ye tell that bastard I'll not stop until every part of their lives, every feckin' Royal Bastard, has been annihilated. The club and all those women and children will become property of the mob. They can try ta run, but I will find them wherever they go."

"Why do you hate them so much?" I ask, as curiosity takes ahold of me. It makes no sense that one man can hate a whole motorcycle club.

"They took everythin' from me. And I'm done playin' games. Don't forget what I said."

He turns and walks out of the pub, leaving me shaking as I glance down at Rogan. His life has been taken by a man who's my own flesh and blood. My uncle saved me.

But this isn't salvation. Patrick Bragan is throwing me into a hell where he sits on the throne.

CHAPTER 11

Sully

The panic that's been twistin' in my gut is enough to have me doubled over in agony. But my focus is on gettin' ta my girl before Rogan does. And if he's already there, I'm goin'ta kill the bastard. I want to see him dead. There's no goin' back fer him. He walked into my city, and I'm goin'ta make sure he doesn't walk back out again.

It doesn't take long fer us to pull up to the bar. I know Clover is inside, but I don't see the two prospects outside. They should have been watchin' the pub fer anyone who matched Rogan's photo that Tye found online. But I don't see them, which only has me worried even more.

I rush up to the door of the pub, but I'm halted in my tracks by shock and surprise the moment I glance through the window.

Fer a moment, I think I'm seein' things, but there's no doubt who the man is standing in front of Clover. I'm torn. Monster and Rebel, and the rest of the brothers, are about to walk in there, and I'm not sure what I'm witnessin'. Both sides of me—brother and lover—wants to do right by the people I love.

Clover has been hidin' things from me, I knew that, but fer her ta not tell me she's acquainted with Bragan is worse than I imagined. She knows him, and I'm pretty sure I know how. They're family. It's probably why she didn't want to talk about her uncle who helped her come over here, who gave her the pub. I didn't look into the deeds of the bar, because I didn't think anythin' of it. I figured family helped family, but this is another level of fecked up.

Bragan turns away from her and makes his way to the rear of the pub as Monster joins me. I glance over my shoulder and find the rest of the brothers headin' fer the back of the premises.

"Is he in there?" Monster asks, capturin' my attention.

"Monster!" Rebel's voice comes from behind the pub where I know Bragan just exited, but I don't say anythin' ta Monster. I can't.

"Come," the man I've known fer most of my life says, and I follow behind as we make our way down the small, cobbled side street that leads to the rear.

I should tell him. Feck. But I can't bring myself to put her in danger. I'd rather put myself in harm's way than allow anythin' ta happen ta Clover. I could lose everythin'. I don't want shite to break down my family, but if the woman I'm fallin' fer walked out on me, I'm not sure what I'd do. I do know I need ta talk to her.

When I was around Clover's father, he never once mentioned a brother, and it makes me wonder if he was tryin'ta hide it from me. If I was a member of Patrick's family, I'd want ta hide it as well. And maybe, just maybe, it's why Clover didn't tell me. She knows how I'd react, and perhaps she's terrified of losin' me.

When we round the back, I meet Bragan's glare. He offers me a knowin' smirk, but he doesn't say anythin' ta me about Clover. I'm grateful because I don't want this bastard tellin' the rest of my brothers about who she is ta him. They're blood relations, and that won't sit well with the rest of the club.

"Finally, the Bastards have caught me," he says as he looks directly at me before flickin' his gaze ta Monster.

"Take him ta the warehouse," Monster says with his fists at his sides. He's ready to attack. I don't blame him.

The rest of the brothers drag Bragan away, but not before he looks directly at me.

"Secrets don't stay buried forever and choices need to be made," he warns me.

And with that, he's taken away, leavin' me with Monster who's watchin' me closely.

"What the feck does he mean by that?" he asks.

I can't lie ta my brother. I can't tell him the truth about Clover either, so I shrug. Headin' ta the bar, I take a deep breath before I walk inside. Monster follows close behind, and I can feel him starin' at my back. He must know somethin' isn't right, but that's one of the things I respect about him—he won't push. He'll wait it out until I come clean.

There, on the floor, is a body, and I have no doubt it's Rogan. But it's only when I look at Clover that panic sets in. She's bleedin' and lookin' weak when I reach her.

"What the feck happened?" I ask, the fear of losin' her is clear in my voice.

"I'm okay," she whispers, but her eyes are flutterin' closed. I didn't notice she was wounded from outside. If I was bein' honest, I was more focused on Bragan than her.

"Take her to the hospital," Monster orders me. "I'll have the prospects come and clean this up." I look up at him, and I want to cry. I haven't done that in years, but I know how lucky I am, havin' him as my best friend. He's never let me down in all the years I've known him, but right now, I'm the one lettin' him down. "Go," he tells me. It's one word, and I don't argue.

Liftin' Clover into my arms, I carry her out into the side street and make my way to the bikes. I'm not sure how the feck to get her on the back of one, so I end up on the main road, hailin' a taxi. The driver looks as panicked as I feel.

When we reach the hospital, I rush Clover into the ER. Even though she's not fatally wounded, she's lost a lot of blood. I'm met by a couple of the nurses who I recognise from when they've stitched either me or one of the brothers up before. They help me get Clover admitted into surgery within minutes.

I don't bother callin' Monster. Mainly because I'm

too feckin' scared he'll figure it all out. My focus is on what Clover's goin' through. I don't know what's goin'ta happen, but as I pace the hospital corridor, waitin' fer news, I realise I'm in love with her.

I don't want her to leave, but I'm not sure how the brothers are going to take her bein' Bragan's niece. Especially when she hid it from me fer months. She coulda told me, but instead, she kept it a secret. I knew there was somethin' off. I just didn't think it would be anythin' like this, though.

Deep down, I wondered if there was a kid she was keepin' from me. I could have handled a kid. Never thought I'd have one, but when I think about Clover carryin' my bairn, I can't deny I'd gladly fill her up every night ta make it happen.

I wonder if Ma would have ever wanted ta be a nan. Back then, I didn't want to consider the possibility. There were too many fecked up arseholes in the world, and I didn't want ta add to that. If they turned out like me, it would be a nightmare. I didn't want ta have a bairn ta worry about. And knowin' where I was headed, joinin' the club, I didn't think I could ever raise a family, let alone have a wife. But Clover fucked all that up because now I can't think of anythin' else.

There are so many things that could go wrong now,

and I don't know if tellin' me the truth is even in her mind. I need her to admit everythin'ta me. I can't live with someone who's goin'ta keep shite secret. Ma used to hide things from Conall, and he would always find out. Her keepin' secrets wasn't right, but what he did ta her was worse. Far feckin' worse. However, I know that hidin' things never helps any situation. I wouldn't ever hurt Clover, but I can't deny I'm feckin' livid she didn't tell me the truth.

Just as I'm about to fetch some coffee from the canteen, Ronan McCallum saunters into the hospital. I want to walk in the opposite direction, to avoid confrontation, but he sees me and makes a feckin' beeline fer me. He must have heard from someone that we have Bragan. I'm not sure what he wants with the arsehole, but he's not goin'ta get him from Monster. There's no way my best friend is goin'ta give up the man he's spent most of his life searchin' fer.

I do find it strange Bragan was so easy to capture. He didn't put up a fight, and he didn't even try to get away. Perhaps he was blindsided that we'd arrived at the bar, or maybe he didn't want McCallum findin' him first. Either way, I'm goin'ta get ta the bottom of this.

"What the feck are ye doin' here?" I demand by way

of greeting.

McCallum doesn't respond fer a while, then he smiles. "I overheard ye've got the wee American girl," he tells me. "And I've also found out the Bastards have got Bragan in their warehouse."

"Aye, there isn't any way ye're goin'ta get ta him now," I tell him.

I'm sure McCallum wants him dead, and he can be certain that Patrick Bragan isn't goin'ta be alive for much longer.

"Oh, I don't want him. I just need ta know he's goin'ta pay fer his sins. And when he does, I'll step up into his shoes." Everything clicks into place as he speaks. The fecker wanted this all along. But there's more ta the story than meets the eye. The glint of satisfaction that's shinin' in his stare sets me on edge.

"What is it ye're not tellin' me?" I don't want to start an altercation in the hospital, even though they've probably seen worse. But if it comes down ta it, I'll feckin' do it.

"There's one tiny problem with my plan," Ronan says. "Yer wee girlfriend needs to go. I can't take over the organisation if she's in the country."

"She's not leavin' fer ye," I tell him as anger takes ahold of me. I'm not lettin' Clover go because of this piece of shite.

"If ye think ye're standin' in my way, Sully, then ye have another thing comin'," he warns, and I can tell he's not givin' this up anytime soon.

"So, ye're plannin' on gettin' rid of all Bragan's family?"

McCallum thinks Clover is a problem, but I don't know if he realises there are two other obstacles in his way—Bragan's daughters—Miren and Callia.

"Aye, if I have ta." He nods. "Tell that wee thing ye've been shaggin' I'm goin'ta make her life a nightmare if she doesn't leave Belfast. I don't need the organisation learnin' who she is."

"Ye said there's an agent in Belfast." When I saw him last, he mentioned an American agent in the country. He must have thought it was Clover. But she's not an agent.

"Aye, there is one," he tells me. "I know it ain't yer girl, though, but she's got somethin' ta do with it, and I will find out what it is." He leans in close, his face in mine. "Get rid of her. She needs to leave soon, or I'll get my boyos ta do the job ye can't."

He doesn't wait for a response. I watch him walk away, while my hands fist at my sides. I'm not sure what the feck is goin' on, but it's time Clover tells me everythin'.

When I finally find coffee, I head back to the waitin' room. This is the worst part about these places. There's nothin' ta do but spend time with yer thoughts. And mine are a feckin' mess right now. I don't know what Clover's been hidin' from me. Her story checked out—her comin' here because she knew her da lived in Ireland when he was a child, and her reachin' out to her uncle because he could help her escape. But if she's workin' with an agent, why didn't they help her?

Nothin' makes sense. I don't understand it, and I need answers. The more I pace back and forth, the more anxious I get. My stomach's in knots by the time the door opens and the doctor walks in.

"She's going to be fine," he tells me. "She's been asking fer ye. We rarely allow non-family members into the rooms, but she says you're the only person she knows here."

"Aye, thanks, Doc," I tell him as he leads me down the long, brightly lit hospital corridor.

I feckin' hate these places. Nothin' good ever comes from bein' in them. I've heard all the heartbreakin' stories about family members havin'ta say goodbye. I never want to experience that kinda grief. It's why I spent most of my younger years on my own, and it's why I choose not to stay at the clubhouse. As much as I love the brothers, I've always distanced myself from emotion, from lovin' people. I'm loyal ta them, I'll die fer them, but I don't know how I'd feel if I were to lose one of them.

And that's what scares the feck out of me.

When I walk into the room, and I see Clover, my chest tightens, because there are more secrets in her eyes than ever before. And she needs ta come clean.

No more hidin'.

CHAPTER 12

Clover

When he walks in, I'm nervous. I can tell from the look on his face, he's not happy. There are so many things I should have told him, but now there's no longer a reason to hide the truth. I've made a decision that, once I get out of here, I'm going home. I can't put him in danger, and I can't hurt him anymore.

Sully deserves so much better than me, and I've put him in a situation where he's going to have to lie to the club. I can't ask him to do that. My lies have finally caught up with me, and I have to pay the price.

"How are ye feelin'?" Sully asks as he settles into the chair beside my bed where I'm sitting up with pillows at my back.

He's so calm, and yet, I know he's hiding rage because it dances in his eyes. He must know everything by now. But he's going to want to hear it from me. I can't believe it's come to this.

I can't believe my uncle allowed himself to be captured. The club now has him, and I've a feeling he did it on purpose. Maybe he wants to be in their possession to stay away from the agency that's after him.

When Sully brought me in, I was feeling dizzy, and I was close to passing out, but so far, I've remained conscious. My wound's been stitched, and I've been given blood to replenish what I lost, so I'm feeling much stronger now.

"I'm okay. I'll live," I tell Sully.

As I stare at him, I can see the questions in his eyes. There are so many, and I'm going to have to answer them all.

"What was Bragan doin' in the pub?" Sully asks.

It's the first of many questions, but it's the most important one. My answer will reveal the one thing I didn't tell him, because I was scared of his reaction. I was too afraid to lose him, so instead of being honest, I hid the truth.

"He's..." I take a long, deep breath, and I close my eyes. The agony of my heart breaking is coursing through me. "He's my uncle."

"Feckin' hell, Clover," Sully says as he runs his fingers through his hair.

He shakes his head, looking at me from under his dark lashes. I've destroyed his trust. It's clear to see in his expression. I never wanted this to happen, but I knew it was inevitable when I didn't tell him the truth. I left it for far too long.

"My father... Dad disowned Patrick when he took over the mob. They hadn't spoken in years, and yet, when I reached out to him, he offered to help me after I arrived in Belfast. I was so scared of Rogan finding me, I agreed to keep his secret." My chest tightens when I consider there's more to the story than I'm telling him, but that will follow. I'm going to have to come completely clean, even though it's against all the rules I've agreed to abide by.

"Ye can't have thought I'd have let ye walk away," Sully says, and I realize just how stupid I've been. Surely if he cared for me, like he so clearly did, he would have kept me safe.

"I've decided to leave," I tell him then. "I have to get back to the States and finish things I started."

This time, Sully looks even more confused. "Ye're mine, Clover," he says to me. "I'm not lettin' ye walk out just like that."

His gaze bores into me. It digs right down into the depths I wanted so badly to hide from him. In the past, Rogan would make me feel less than a woman, but with Sully, he's always lifted me up. He's always given me the confidence to be stronger, and I can't believe it's come to this.

"Sully, you have to listen to me, please. There are things I need to mend back home, but..." I shake my head. "I'll be safe because Rogan is dead. When Patrick killed him, he told me to leave you and the club. And I have a feeling, even though your club have him in their custody, this isn't over."

I came to Ireland because it was an escape, but then I recall the meeting I had just before I got on the flight. When the agency saw my name, they realized I was the only way to track down the man they'd been looking for.

Even though Dad hated Patrick, he never agreed to rat on his brother. And as much as the CIA wanted

Patrick Bragan, my father wouldn't budge. There wasn't much they could do. Dad always stayed on the right side of the law. He didn't deal with anything illegal, so they couldn't threaten him with prison. So, they waited. For me.

"Ye're workin' with the agent who's in the city. Aren't ye?" Sully says, surprising me. I didn't think he knew. "Ronan McCallum was here. He wants me to tell ye ta leave Belfast because he doesn't want anyone in the way of him steppin' into yer uncle's shoes. He wants the mob fer himself."

It's all not news to me. "I know," I whisper, and I watch as the realization slowly creases his expression. "I wanted to tell you so many times, but—"

"Ye left me in the dark while I was tryin'ta keep ye safe," Sully grits through his teeth as he pins me with a glare.

I don't blame him for being angry. He should be because I didn't give him all of me. I held back.

"I wanted to keep you safe, Sully. The deeper I got into this, the more I was worried that Patrick would hurt you. There was nothing I could do but follow the rules set out by the agent, in the hope it would keep you out of harm's way."

As Sully paces, he clenches his hands into fists at his

sides. His knuckles are white as he presses his nails into his palms. I want so much to go to him, to touch him and calm him down, but I know it won't work. There are waves of panic washing through me, and as I scoot up in the bed, I can't help but wince as the stitches tug at my skin.

Sully notices and rushes to my side. "Ye need ta sit back. Don't move until the doctor tells ye it's okay."

Even in his anger, in his frustration, he's caring for me. I should never have lied to him, hid things from him. There's no doubt in my mind I've messed this up, and I know there's no going back now.

"After everything, I think it's for the best that I head back to the States. It will give us both some time to consider how we feel about what's happened. I need to get a flight and go home," I tell him, and as I say the words, I realize it's another lie. I'm not really going *home*, because that's with Sully now. But if I tell him how I feel while he's so angry, he'll never let me go.

"So ye're just goin'ta walk away?" he challenges me, and I nod.

I can't find words to explain, to answer him, so all I do is turn my gaze away from his. My chest is tight, and my heart is in my throat as I fight back the tears.

"I don't think I have a choice, Sully. There are so

many things I need to sort out back in White Pass. I have to see Darius and talk to him. I have to decide where my future lies." All of my confession is done without meeting those dark eyes I've come to love. Every part of Sully is mine, and I want so much to be his, but I have to fix the mess I left back home.

"If I was ta come with ye," Sully says. "I would have ta choose between ye and my brothers. I don't know how ta do that." His honesty steals my breath. My chest is aching. I want so much to heal him, to fix what I've broken.

"I won't ever ask you to do that." My voice breaks when I speak. "I know I was the one who messed up, and it's a decision I'm going to have to live with. I don't expect you to choose me, to want me, or to come after me. When I leave, I'm saying goodbye."

Sully meets my watery gaze, but he doesn't make a move to come to me. I miss him already. I miss his arms around me, keeping me safe. But I don't think I could handle it if he did hold me. I'd break down, and I don't want him to see me like that.

I can't breathe. It feels like I'm about to shatter in half. And I know it's going to ruin me when I finally have to walk away from him.

"Thank you for everything you've ever done for me,

Sully. You healed me when I was at my most broken, and I can never change how I feel about you, but I know it is best for me to leave."

Sully shakes his head, and looks away from me, before moving to the window. Silence hangs heavily between us in the room, and I don't break it. I can't. The lump in my throat threatens to choke me when I think about walking away from him, but I can't stay.

"I have to go and talk to Darius. There are things I need to tie up with him taking over the club," I whisper, fighting back the tears that are burning my eyes.

Guilt twists in my gut, and I watch his shoulders tense as he stares out at the view from the room.

"Then ye'll have ta go. Once yer discharged from here, I'll take ye to the airport." He sighs, and shaking his head, he makes his way to the door. "I'll wait on ye."

As the door shuts behind him, I finally allow the tears to fall. I didn't want him to see me like this, but there's no longer a way to stop the pain coursing through me. When the door opens again, I expect it to be him, but instead, it's the doctor who offers me a gentle smile.

"Miss Byrne," he says as he stops at my bedside.

"Doctor, I would really like to go home. I can't stay here for much longer." He thinks I'm talking about the hospital, instead, I mean Belfast. There's not much for me to do at the club back home. But I needed to tell Sully something. He should let me go because I've only brought lies to his door when he didn't deserve it.

The doctor opens the manila folder in his hand and scans the details before nodding. "Everything looks good. You have lost a lot of blood, and you will feel weak fer a wee while yet. The transfusion will help, but you need to rest. I'll have a nurse come in to remove the drip shortly."

"Thank you, I appreciate it."

"You're welcome to go home in the morning, but only if there is someone who can look after ye there," he tells me with a stern look on his face.

"Yes, doctor, I understand." I nod, but I don't tell him that I'm going to have to fly soon. I'll be okay, I'm sure I will. He makes a few notes on the paperwork in the folder before offering me a smile and leaving the room with a quiet *goodbye*. And then I'm alone with my thoughts.

I allow my mind to drift back to the day at the airport when I almost ran from the agent who was trying to get me to listen to her.

"You're Clover Byrne," she says as I pick up my coffee

and try to make a hasty retreat. "I need you to listen to me, Clover." She settles in the seat across from me and sets down a folder.

Panic sets in as I look at her. "I don't want any trouble. There are things I'm trying to get away from. I need to find safety."

"We can ensure your safe passage out of the country, if you help us."

I shake my head in disbelief as I wonder what the hell is even happening. How is it she could just come up to me in the middle of a fucking airport?

I meet her stare and whisper, "How did you find me?"

She smiles. "We've been watching the club for years, but when you left, we couldn't track you until we found some hospital records that were sent through to us. We'd been looking in the wrong place for you. We wanted your father to help us, but he was never willing to give up his brother. If you work for us, we can make sure you're looked after when you return to the States." I realize it could be a good deal because I don't know if I'll want to live in Belfast forever. But, can I work undercover?

I take in her outfit. She looks like an office worker in her dark pants suit. The ID she sets on the table has her photo, name, and the official-looking stamp of the agency. I've never seen anything like it in real life, only ever in movies.

"It seems your boyfriend kept you under wraps. While we were searching for you in one place, he'd been covering his tracks and yours."

I've no doubt in my mind that Rogan was making sure nobody knew about the abuse. He always ensured I'd cover up any visible injuries when we went out after he lost his mind, but I didn't realize he was hiding all my hospital records as well.

"The thought of doing something like this makes me nervous. I just want to leave the country. And get away from my ex." My voice shudders when I speak. "I don't want to get involved with anything that could put me back into danger. I'm finally escaping a horrible life, and I don't want more." I explain my situation while looking at her.

"I'm sorry to hear that." Her voice lowers. "We can keep you safe from him. I promise you that. There's no reason to fear him anymore."

"I'm sure there are plenty of reasons why my father chose not to help you. And honestly, I don't want to get involved in whatever it is you're proposing."

I push to my feet, but she stops me with a gentle hand on my shoulder.

"We just need you to gather information, and when you do, send it through to me. I'll be landing in Belfast not long after you, so I'll be close by if you need anything. We can't do *this without you. Patrick Bragan is not a good man, Clover."*

"He's my uncle," I tell her, and she nods. It's something she already knows. "And you say my dad didn't want to do this?"

She shakes her head. "No. He refused to betray his brother, even though they weren't close. We want to get the head of the Irish mob, Clover, and you're the only one who can help."

Dad never spoke much about his brother. There were times I would ask about his life in Ireland, but he told me he didn't want to look back at the past. And I respected that. I only knew of Patrick because I found his details in Dad's papers after he died. And when I reached out to Uncle Patrick, he told me he'd look after me.

"Okay, I'll do it," I finally say.

"Here's a folder. It will give you all the details you need. Read through it on the flight," she says as she hands me the documents. "If you need anything, my number is in there. And here's a burner phone. Don't let anyone get ahold of this. We'll be able to track you with it, and make sure you're safe at all times."

I don't know why I'm agreeing to this. It may not be the best idea, but it's something I can do to refocus myself. I ran from Rogan, and if they can keep me safe from him, then perhaps it's all for the best.

"Thanks."

That wasn't the last time I heard from her. And I've emailed her everything I could find so far. But now the club has Patrick, and I'm not sure what they plan to do with him. The agency wanted the head of the mob, but like Sully said, Ronan McCallum plans to take over, so maybe they'll want him instead.

Now I'm going to have to go back to the States and face the club. I'll have to say goodbye to Sully. And as the realization hits me, I can't stop the tears from falling again.

CHAPTER 13

Sully

When I open my eyes, I sigh when I realise where I am. The hospital waitin' room is quiet, with only myself spread across the small leather sofa. I didn't want ta see her again, so I chose to wait here until she was discharged.

The doctor mentioned he'd given her the go ahead to leave today, rather than last night. But he did tell me ta watch over her as she'll still be weak from the blood loss. If I could keep her here, I would. But I'll never force a woman ta do anythin' she doesn't want ta.

I'm not angry anymore. When Clover first admitted the truth ta me, I was livid, but as I stand here in the hospital, I realise she's always been mine. And even though she didn't tell me the whole truth, she's still mine.

Her decision to leave is a shock ta me. I don't want her ta go. But I also know there are things I need ta sort out here. With Bragan in our possession, I'm goin'ta have ta be there fer the brothers and the club.

I love her, and I want nothin' more than ta have her live with me, wakin' up with her every mornin'. But perhaps havin' some space between us may help. It will give us a fresh perspective.

Her flat is quiet when we walk in. I can feel the tension emanatin' off her as she goes ta the bedroom ta pack her bags. I don't offer ta help, but I watch her from the open-plan lounge.

She stops fer a moment and looks over at me.

"I didn't mean for this to happen, Sully."

I can tell she's sorry. She regrets hidin' things from me.

"We all make our own choices," I tell her.

I don't offer her any words of forgiveness, even though I'm worried about her and don't want to let her go. And it makes me wonder if Monster felt like this about Miren when he found out her truth.

Clover nods and continues packin' as I settle at the kitchen counter. When she finally comes into the room and sets the bag down, we stand in silence. I want ta pull her into my arms. I never expected to feel this pain, but she's become a part of my life. There's no way ta get her out of my heart, because she's burrowed herself right the feck in there.

"I don't want ye ta do this," I tell her finally. I need her ta know I'm not happy she's leavin'. "Goin' back there," I continue when she doesn't respond. "You belong here, Clover."

Slowly, she lifts her gaze to mine and nods. She knows she belongs ta me. There's no denyin' it.

"This is something I have to do," she says, her voice crackin' on the words as she blinks back the tears. "Please, just let me go. I want to focus on fixing things back home. And if, after a bit, you're still in the mindset you want me, you can come and find me."

This is the first time she's said that, and it settles my anxiety, somewhat. I still don't feel as if she should go. But, I will respect her wishes. I know I can't force her to stay. I'll give her the space she's askin' fer. It won't be fer very long, though.

"Fair enough," I tell her. "I've walked away from ye before, though," I continue. "And I don't know if I want ta do it again."

Clover offers me a gentle smile, one that makes her eyes sparkle when she looks at me. "You're a good person," she tells me. "And I believe that happiness will find you. There are so many things we've been through, and I'm thankful I found you."

"And you're still goin'ta leave," I throw back as frustration takes over. I shouldn't allow myself ta be angry. My feckin' feelin's are all over the place.

"It doesn't have to be forever," she says softly. "We need some space." She's right, but I don't want ta admit it. "I didn't want to lie to you, to hide anything from you."

"I know, sweetheart," I tell her as I pull her into my arms. It's the first time since the hospital I've touched her. And it feels good to have her in my arms again. "I respect your decision. I don't have ta like it, though."

"I know," Clover mumbles into my chest, but she snuggles herself in and holds onto me as if I'm a lifeline and she's drownin'. "It's not forever."

"It's not," I agree. "Because I will come fer ye when I can." It's a promise I make as I lead her down to the SUV.

I couldn't take her on the bike with her luggage, so I borrowed the vehicle from the club. I have to head back after droppin' Clover at the airport and talk ta Monster. I'm not entirely sure what he's goin'ta say ta me, but I'm hopin' he's not goin'ta hate Clover fer what she did.

The drive is filled with silence as we make our way through the city and towards the airport. With every mile, the more my anxiety twists in my gut. At least I know that when Clover gets home, she won't have to worry about that bastard Rogan bein' there, waitin' fer her.

Pullin' into the airport parkin' garage, I kill the engine and sit back. There's time before her flight takes off, so I don't move until I know what I want ta say.

"I've been angry," I tell her then, but I don't look at her. I keep my stare on the windscreen in front of me. "When I knew you lied, hid somethin' from me, it hit me harder than I expected. I didn't think I could ever feel this with anyone. But now you're leavin', I can tell ye fer sure. I'm in love with ye."

Silence greets me, but I don't expect her to say anythin'. I needed her ta know I'm not someone who's goin'ta walk away from her, and I'm not goin'ta just accept her decision as final. We may need time to fix shite, but there's no chance I'm goin'ta lose her forever.

"When ye're ready," I continue. "I want ye to call me. Tell me how ye're feelin'. I want to know how ye're doin'. I want ta be the first person ye call on when ye're ready to live again because I want us to be together."

Clover shifts in her seat, and I glance over at her. She's lookin' at me with those pretty eyes, and I know I'm goin'ta miss them. She has this silent softness in her stare that makes me feel like a feckin' hero. Even though I know I'm not. Far from it. But Clover looks at me like I'm the man she loves.

We get out of the car and head into the building, and I realise this is it. I'm goin'ta have ta say goodbye ta her. There are people waitin' on their flight numbers gettin' called, and I want to tell Clover I'm goin' with her. But I can't. She needs ta do this, and I can't stop her. There's nothin' I can do to keep her here, short of feckin' tyin' her ta my bed.

When we reach her gate, I wait with her in silence. There's nothin' I can say to her now. I've told her I love her. And it wasn't a lie. It's the first time I've said it to someone in a long feckin' time.

It's been a lifetime since I offered my heart to anyone. When I was in school, I thought I loved someone. But it was nothin' more than a teenage crush.

I didn't know what genuine love was back then. All the women since have been one-night stands. They've meant nothin' ta me. But when Clover walked into my life, shite changed. She feckin' changed me.

"I have to go," Clover whispers softly, and I look down at her.

Her gate and flight number are bein' called. Once she walks through those doors, I won't see her again. I won't wake up ta her, and I won't be fallin' asleep beside her. The idea of losin' her makes my gut churn. I don't like it. But I know it's fer the best. Fer now.

"Aye," I say as I cup her face in my hands. "Once I've helped Monster deal with Bragan, I'll come fer ye." There's no lie in my words, and I hold her gaze hostage. She has to know I'm not lyin'. "I meant what I said to ye, Lucky," I tell her as I lean in and press my lips to hers. Her sweetness settles on my tongue, and it courses through my veins.

When I finally pull away, there are tears in her eyes. I don't want to see her cry, so I look away and release her from my hold.

"Have a safe flight," I say to her, and I offer a nod, which she doesn't see because she can't even look at me. We're all done now. This is it. "Call me when ye're home. I just need ta know ye're safe. Okay?"

"I will," she promises, but I have a feelin' she won't.

Deep down, I'm convinced this could be the last time I'll ever see this girl. Even though I know where her club is at White Pass. Somethin' tells me Clover is tryin' ta escape. She's so used ta runnin' away, she's doin' it with me as well. She doesn't know what I'm like, though. I don't give up so easily.

I watch her go. And I can't deny my eyes burn with unshed feckin' tears. My long hair hangs loose around my face, and it covers the emotion I'm tryin'ta hide from the people passin' me by.

I turn and head back to the SUV. Once inside, I sit quietly and stare at the road just outside the garage. The view distracts me from the thoughts racing through my head. Leanin' my head back on the car seat, I focus on the roof of the feckin' vehicle instead. Everythin' is goin'ta remind me of her.

There's no escapin' what Clover has done ta me. And seein' her walk away was too feckin' much fer me. I start the engine and make my way back ta the club. There's only one man who'll understand, and it's Monster.

When I finally pull into the drive of the clubhouse, I'm met by the man I need ta talk to. I exit the vehicle and throw the keys his way. He catches them with the expertise of a sportsman.

"Ye goin'ta tell me what the feckin' hell is goin' on?" Monster says as he grips my shoulder and leads me towards church.

Our meetin' room is a safe haven where we're able to talk honestly. And it's time fer me ta come clean. He doesn't know everythin' yet. Bragan is still in our warehouse, but I've a feelin' he won't be breathin' fer much longer.

There's goin'ta be a few interrogation sessions before his life comes to an end, though, and I'm goin'ta have ta clean up the mess. I settle into a chair while Monster takes the head of the table. It's where I first watched him take over from his Da.

"Tell me everythin'," Monster says as he leans back in his chair. His dark eyes are on me as he waits for the story.

I never thought I would be here, havin' ta defend Clover, havin' ta tell him all of what she's told me. But I know there's no goin' back.

"Clover's gone back to the States," I tell him first. "She's across the pond and there's nothin' I can do."

Monster leans forward, his forearms on the table, as he regards me before askin', "Why?"

"Clover's uncle is Patrick Bragan," I admit quickly, before I can stop myself. "She didn't know him growin' up, but when she needed help, he offered. I think the only reason he did was because he hoped she'd get ta me, or one of us at least. But what he doesn't know is she's been helpin' the CIA."

Monster sits back at this news, but he doesn't say anythin'. I didn't expect him to be so calm, but then again, Monster is someone who thinks about things before reactin'.

"She's gone back home to sort shite out," I confirm.

He looks at me. "Do ye love her?" This is a question I wasn't expectin', but one I know I need ta answer. Not only fer him, but fer myself too.

I pause before I reply. Even though I told her how I felt, I don't know if I thought everythin' through. Clover's been keepin' secrets that should never have been kept.

Sighin', I finally look at Monster and nod. "Aye, I feckin' love her. She's my world. My everythin'."

He looks at me then. There's more emotion in his eyes than he's ever offered any of the other brothers. Then he clears his throat, and I realise he's about to say something profound.

"Ye know, when Miren came into my life, I hated

her because she was the blood of Bragan. She wasn't just family, she was his daughter. And I didn't think there was anythin' that could make me change my mind about her."

"But you're married now." It's a thought that's plagued me.

If he can accept Miren, surely he can accept Clover. She's a good girl, she'd never let me down.

"Aye, I am. And I don't think ye walkin' away from the woman ye love is a good idea. Once ye're in love, there's nothin' that will change it. And ye can't fight that shite. No matter how hard ye try ta."

"So what do I do?" I ask him, knowing he'll offer me sound advice.

Trust hasn't been the easiest thing for me to give. But with Monster, it came easily when I learned that he was brutally honest. He would always tell me the truth. I thought he wouldn't want Clover in the clubhouse again, but he seems to be calm about it. More so than I was. More than I expected him ta be.

"Give her the time she needs," Monster advises, "But don't leave it too long. Ye need her to know ye love her."

I offer him a smile, and say, "Then let's question Bragan and get this done. I'm not leavin' ye ta deal with

this alone. Once I know it's all sorted, I'll go to her."
And I realise I'm not lyin'. I do love that girl, and I'm
goin'ta go ta her. She may have left, but it's not the end
for us. It can't be.

"One thing I've learned," Monster says, "never give
up on somethin' that makes ye feel alive. It's worth the
risk. And ye need ta trust yer feelin's. And if ye tell
anyone I ever feckin' said that, I'll deny it."

It's times like this I'm reminded of just how much
this man loves me. We're brothers. We may not have
the same blood coursin' through our veins, but we're
family. And nothin' is ever goin'ta change it.

It's all set then. As soon as this shite with Bragan is
done, I'll go ta Clover. I'll go claim my girl.

CHAPTER 14

Two months later

Life back in the States has been strange, to say the least. I didn't think coming back here alone would be something I could ever do.

I didn't want to leave Sully, but I knew after all the lies I needed to give him space. Walking away from someone I love wasn't easy, and there's no way I can forget all the good times I had with him. The feelings that grew between us are still there. They will always be there.

He healed me in ways I didn't expect. He mended the parts of me that were still broken, still wounded from Rogan's abuse. And even though I've only got one scar that hasn't been covered with ink, I know where the rest are hiding. My choice not to cover the knife wound Rogan's blade gave me was to prove my strength. I wanted to remember the moment I was ready to die. All the years of thinking about it, it was only in that moment I would've gladly given my life for Sully's. I knew if he'd walked into the pub right then, Rogan would have attacked him, but I knew deep down Rogan would have been happy with me dead. So, I chose to die to keep Sully safe. And then, Bragan's gunshot saved me.

I don't know where I would be if it weren't for Patrick, and I don't know what happened to him, but I have a feeling he's also met his maker.

The Bastards wouldn't have spared him, and I'm not at all sorry for that. He didn't deserve to live. I've since learned more about the things he's done over the years. Darius mentioned things my father kept from me, and now I know why Dad walked out on him. Patrick was an evil man. A villain in a story where the hero doesn't wear shining armor, but a leather cut instead.

The sun is high in the cloudless sky when I step out of the house. My father left all this to me, and even though he's gone, I have a home, and I have the brothers who care for me as if I were their daughter. From the moment I walked back into the clubhouse, they accepted me.

Since my return, I've allowed Darius to keep running the club, but I sit in on church, learning about the daily goings on. It's been a good thing for me to do because now I can see why Dad loved these men as if they were blood. Even though there's only one man who will forever hold my heart, the brothers have been there to help me get back on my feet. They are my family, and I couldn't have survived these last couple of months without them.

"Clover girl," Ahren walks up the drive towards me. He's been with the club for a long while. I was a kid when he first patched in, and now he's taken over as the VP for the Kovenant. "Are you okay?"

He stops in front of me and looks me over. I've been thankful for his friendship. He reminds me of Tye in many ways. He's still one of the youngest members of our club, but he's also one of the most tech savvy. He's involved in the hacking side of the business, finding information on those we need to track down. I'm sure he'll be running his own office soon, just like Tye.

"Hey, don't get stuck in your head about things," he tells me. "I know you like to get lost in the past. Remember, you're here with us now. And there's nothing you can do to change what happened."

Nodding, I whisper, "Yeah, I know. It's just difficult, knowing I can't fix all the shit that went down. There'll never be a time I can come back from that. I lied to Sully, and I don't blame him if he never wants to seem me again."

"The thing about it is, darling, if Sully truly loves you, then the forgiveness you seek will come. He's been hurt, and maybe he just needs more time. Give him that because he's offered you the space you asked for."

There's a calmness to Ahren's words and his gaze. I wish I could believe him, but it's been half a year, and I've had no contact from Sully, or any of his brothers. I never expected him to forgive me, because I lied to him for far too long, but I had hoped he'd still want a connection.

"It's been two months," I say finally as my voice breaks, and I can feel the tears burning my eyes. "I just don't think he's going to come back to me."

Ahren offers me a smile and places a hand on my shoulder. The gentle touch is not new to me anymore. The men who live around me now are my safe haven.

"Have faith, Clover girl," Ahren tells me and pulls me into his arms.

For the first time in a long while, I allow myself to fully rest my head on someone else's chest, other than Sully's. The last man I allowed this close was the one who still holds my heart. And now he's not here. At least I feel safe with Ahren.

A few bikes roll up the drive. The rumble of their engines is loud as they near the area where the rest of the brothers park their bikes. I know the club will be busy tonight because they have church.

Ahren doesn't let me go. He knows how I feel about Sully. I was a mess when I arrived back here, and it hasn't been easy. Slowly, my head is coming to terms with the fact I've lost the man I love. But my heart will never believe it. I know that.

"Get yer feckin' hands off her," the deep Irish brogue rumbles through me, and Ahren freezes before he releases me from his hold.

I step back in surprise, and looking over Ahren's shoulder, I come face to face with the man who's had my heart since I was fifteen.

Ahren leans in and whispers, "Have faith, darling." Then he leaves us in the warm sunshine of White Pass.

Sully and I stand in silence, watching each other as if we're both in shock. Perhaps we are. The corner of his mouth tips upwards, and he offers me one of his side smiles.

"You're here," I whisper as I lower my gaze to my shoes. "I didn't think I'd ever see you again and—"

I stop my words when Sully reaches for my chin. Gripping it gently, he lifts my head so I can't look away. His eyes bore into me.

"I figured somethin' out," Sully rumbles in his broad Irish accent.

The tone of his voice causes a shiver to race down my spine. Memories I've tried to tamp down seem to spark up right from my very core.

"What's that?" My words are raspy as I try to swallow back the lump in my throat.

"I can't live without ye," he tells me while he holds my stare hostage with those dark brown eyes. "It's taken me far too feckin' long to find ye, and I'm not prepared to walk away from this again."

"It's been eight long, lonely weeks, Sully."

This time, the tears I've been holding back burn my eyes as they sit on my lashes. I don't want to cry. I've fought long and hard not to break down over the past few months, but now I can't stop the tears from falling. Sully is here.

"I needed to fix myself before I could even think about comin' here to see ye," he says. "Ye're my wee lass, and I don't want to lose ye. I should have come sooner, but the club needed me, and in the end, I chose to stay with them," Sully continues as he looks down at me. There's a smile tugging on his lips that makes me grin and nod. "I had to help them with Bragan, but Monster told me I had ta come out here and find ye. There's no way I'm lettin' ye go. I never could leave ye, believe me."

"I do believe you because that's how I feel. I know I walked away, but we both needed time," I tell him. "I never hated you. My own actions hurt me, and I know I was in the wrong. Deep down, I knew I should've told you the truth from the beginning, but I was too scared of losing you, not realizing I was going to lose you anyway."

A sob threatens to choke me as I try to hold back my pain. Sully doesn't reply, but he pulls me into his arms and cocoons me in his warmth.

"I'm not losin' ye, Lucky." The use of his nickname for me makes me smile as I sob into his chest.

There's a softness to his leather cut. I grip it with

both hands and hold on to him as if he's my lifeline. He's given me the freedom from my past I've been longing for. I can finally move on and allow myself to look to the future.

Sully steps back, and he cups my face in his large, firm hands, his thumbs swiping at my cheeks.

"I'm yours," he tells me as he leans in to press his lips to mine. "Don't ye ever think I'm goin' anywhere." His voice is filled with the confidence I've longed to hear.

"Since the day it all blew up, I've been broken," I mumble as I look up at him.

"Then let me put yer pieces back together, sweetheart," Sully says as he keeps my gaze hostage.

My heart skips a beat as his words settle inside me. They're more than just words, though. There isn't a lie in his eyes. And I finally believe he's truly here to stay. It feels as if it's a dream. At last, I can settle down and allow my happiness to take ahold of me.

"Want to come inside?" I look up at him as I put some space between us.

Sully nods. "Aye, I'm thinkin' of stayin' fer a wee while, if ye'll have me." He laces his fingers with mine, and I drag him into the clubhouse. I can't let him go again, never again.

"I don't want you to leave," I tell him as we make our

way upstairs.

A flutter of excitement and anticipation tumbles in my stomach as we reach my bedroom. It's the same one I've had since I was a teen. The room where I used to fantasize about Sully when I was still a young girl.

Sully shuts the door behind him and tugs me back until my body is flush against his. He doesn't move, neither do I, but his arms wrap around me, and he holds me close. His beard tickles my cheek as his lips trail down to my neck. He captures the sensitive flesh between his teeth before he bites down gently.

"Ye're mine, Lucky," he tells me, the whisper tickling my neck, causing me to tremble in his hold.

I didn't expect things to work out. However, now I'm here, I'm letting my guard down. I don't want to push Sully away, and I need to believe him when he tells me how he feels. Things may have been an up and down roller coaster, but now I'm sure we're on a smoother path.

"I am yours," I say as I turn in his arms to finally meet his gaze. "I've been yours for far longer than you thought."

"Aye." This time, he gives me a mischievous smile that causes me to giggle. "Is this the bedroom where my wee Clover would lie in bed at night and think of me?"

He allows his gaze to flick around the room, and I can't stop the blush that warms my cheeks when I realize he knows. There's no more reason for me to lie to him, to hide anything from him, so I nod.

"Yeah," I finally say as I step back and allow him to explore the space. It's my safe haven, it truly is.

He walks to the window, then over to the closet, before stopping at the side of the bed. Sully looks like a giant in my teenage bedroom.

"It's very like ye," he says before glancing toward me. "And how many times did ye think about me while ye slept here?"

This time, his eyes darken slightly as he regards me. The husky tone of his voice sends warmth coursing through me. I watch as he kicks off his boots and then settles on the mattress with his back against the headboard and legs crossed at the ankles.

I take in the man with the long hair, the beard, and those dark eyes. His jeans fit him perfectly, just like always. His fingers tangle in his lap, and I notice how his arms bulge and strain against the material of his T-shirt.

"A few." I can't help but mumble my reply because I'm embarrassed he knows what I did.

There were nights I would close my eyes and think about the stranger who visited. It was in those moments I lost myself to pleasure while wishing that one day I'd be with him. The man of my dreams.

"Come here, Lucky," he commands in a tone that tells me not to argue.

My feet carry me effortlessly to where he's lying, and I kick my own shoes off as Sully offers me a hand. I accept, and as I tangle my fingers with his, he pulls me toward him until I'm straddling his hips.

Even though we're both in jeans, I can feel his hardness, and I'm pretty sure he can feel my warmth. There's no denying that we missed each other. But he doesn't rush. There are gentle touches as his fingertips trail down my bare arms, causing goosebumps to rise over every inch of me. There's no fighting what's about to happen, and I realize there's no denying our love any longer.

Slowly, teasingly, he hooks his thumbs into the straps of my tank top and pushes them off my shoulders. The material slips down over my curves, and my skin blazes from the look in his eyes. Desire-filled warmth emanates from him, and I lean down to press my lips to his.

"Ye're an exquisite wee thing, Lucky," Sully mumbles

against the corner of my mouth. Then, his fingers tangle in my hair, and he pulls my head back before he finally attacks my neck. He kisses, bites, and sucks the flesh hard until I'm whimpering, and I realize I'm grinding against his crotch.

Sully doesn't speak as he moves his lips down from my neck to my exposed nipple and captures the hardened bud into his mouth. I squeal when his teeth graze along the sensitive peak, and I whimper when he suckles it gently to soothe the bite. His beard sends tingles through every inch of me as I tremble in his arms.

He looks up at me, a small smile tilting his perfectly full lips. "I think I need ta remind ye who ye belong to. Don't I, wee thing?"

EPILOGUE

Clover

Over the years, I've learned how temporary life is. We all walk through life thinking we have time. Most people believe tomorrow will come, and for most, it does. But we can't tell the future. We don't know when we'll take our final breaths. I've come to realize the most important thing is to live your life so that when you're gone, you are remembered by those left behind. Remembered with love and affection because that will leave a legacy for years to come.

Nothing in this world is assured. No matter how

carefully you live your life, it's not guaranteed to always keep you safe. My father believed you had to live each day as if it was your last. Pushing Sully away made me see he wasn't going anywhere. He knocked down walls to keep me from making a mistake. Even though he killed, he did it for a good reason. That's how I look at it. He wanted to save his mother from being hurt, and in my book, that makes him a noble man.

Life has forced me to face the truth—love is unconditional.

I glance out of the window and see the men all looking smart. It makes me smile. The Royal Bastards look so handsome as they stand there in their leather cuts and black denim jeans. And I can only imagine how breathtaking Sully must look in his similar outfit. It's a rehearsal for tomorrow when I'll walk down the aisle and recite my vows.

I walked out of this life when I was younger. My father left a club to me, and I didn't want it. Yet, here I am, walking back into one. Only this time I'm not alone.

The man I'm marrying tomorrow is not like the one that I've run from in the past. Sully is nothing like Rogan. Which is a good thing because I don't think I would be able to survive going through something like that ever again.

I turn and head for the door. Taking the stairs, I smile when I reach the entrance hall where friends are still arriving for the party. It's only a rehearsal, but the house is full. I head outside to where the Royal Bastards have congregated, and my eyes seek out the man who's captured my heart.

"You're perfect," Sully says to me as I stop beside him.

The roar of the bikes is deafening when he leans in to kiss me. It's not even our wedding day, yet they're as excited as we are.

I made the choice to move here permanently, and the club has welcomed me into their family. I was lucky enough to have a wonderful father until he was taken from me. I had the unconditional love of a parent, which is what every child should have, but I never felt fully myself when I was back in the States. It wasn't as if I'd found love or true happiness there.

Since being here, becoming part of the Royal Bastards, I've allowed myself to love, to feel happiness, and to finally let go of the past. There are no more secrets between Sully and me because we've learned they always have a way of revealing themselves. And they have a way of breaking something that's good.

Sully

Marriage.

I don't know what the feck I'm doin'. This isn't where I saw my life goin'. Not ever. The rest of the brothers are all fer it, and I'm here shitting myself. Monster has taken the plunge, and so has Tye, but the rest of us are single. Even though things have been goin' well with Clover, I'm still feckin' nervous.

I shrug on my cut and look at my reflection. I'm goin'ta be a husband today. I don't know how ta do this, but I'm takin' the feckin' chance. Monster told me it's goin'ta be fine, but deep down, I'm a feckin' mess.

When I turn towards the exit, I find Monster standin' there, leanin' against the door frame.

"Do I look okay?" I ask him as I glance down at my white shirt, black jeans, and leather cut. We always wear our leathers, no matter what.

"Aye, ye look like a man about ta marry the woman you love," he tells me with a chuckle. "Ye know, I didn't think ye'd ever be takin' this step, but when I see ye with her, I can tell there's nothin' ye're hidin' anymore. Ye've come a long way, Sully."

Even though we're the same age, Monster speaks ta me as if he were the older brother, offerin' advice. But at the moment, it's what I need. He has more experience in this than I do. He's been married now fer a wee while, and he knows what it's like.

"I never expected ta want her as much as I do. And it's not just the intimacy, it's the feckin' way she makes me feel like I'm her Prince feckin' Charming."

"Aye, they have a way of doin' that ta ye." He shakes his head, and from the knowin' smile on his face, it's clear Miren makes him feel exactly the same. "Ready?"

"Aye." I nod, and we make our way out ta the clubhouse grounds. The gardens are lush today, with the sun shinin' brightly, and the cloudless sky is so blue it's blindin'.

It doesn't take long fer the bridesmaids ta walk down the makeshift aisle. There are only four of them, includin' Miren. They're all wearin' champagne coloured dresses, and as they line up facin' us lads, I can't help but grin. It's a beautiful sight. Everyone together.

And that's when the music changes, and I see her. Clover's dress is a soft cream colour. The lace that lines her torso has small green gemstones that shimmer each time she moves. The sun catches the material makin' her look like she's a jewel movin' towards me.

When she comes to a stop in front of me, I'm at a loss fer words. There's nothin' I can say ta her that will do her justice. She's incredible. I don't know how I got this lucky, but she certainly has brought good fortune to my life.

"We are gathered here today to bring together Sully Murphy and Clover Byrne. They've both written their own promises to recite. Clover, would you like to start?"

My girl nods and she looks up at me, her eyes shimmerin', and I'm pretty feckin' sure I'm about ta start cryin' too.

"I didn't think a happy ever after was in the cards for me, but then you came along. A storm of a man, and a hero in my eyes. You stole my pain, my heartbreak, and my distrust, and you replaced them with happiness, love, and loyalty. You've given me a safe haven in your arms, and a home in your heart. And I know it's where I will always stay. Happiness isn't what you have, what you own, it's who loves you, and I know I'm both lucky and happy to have you."

Clearin' my throat, I swallow back the emotion

that's so foreign ta me, and I smile. I don't know how my vows will top that, but I'm goin'ta feckin' try.

"Today, I stand here a new man. There were times I didn't think I could love, because I didn't want ta risk ever losin' that person. But you taught me ta see the light, ta stop waitin' fer the sadness ta come, and instead, ta grab the happiness with both hands and hold on to it. I promise ye, my lucky Clover, that from this day forward, I'll be there fer ye. I'll be the hero you never had before, and I'll be the man who makes ye proud every feckin' day."

"Thank you, both," Father Halloran says. "It's time fer the rings."

As our vows are made, we slide the rings on each other's fingers, and the father pronounces we're husband and wife. I sweep Clover into my arms and kiss her until we're both breathless.

And I know that my forever has just begun.

If you're in a situation similar to Clover was, please reach out to the following people in your country:

UK: <u>REFUGE</u>
US: <u>THE HOTLINE</u>
CA: <u>SHELTERSAFE.CA</u>
AU: <u>1800 RESPECT</u>
SA: <u>TEARS</u>

SNEAK PEEK

Rebel

The Past

I think about death a lot. Far more than anyone my age should. Mid-twenties, in good health, no reckon' ailments to speak of, and yet, the idea of dying is on my mind all the time.

I am convinced my father was the one who caused those thoughts to invade my mind. I watched him kill. Since I was young enough to remember, there was never a time Da didn't have blood on his hands. He'd come home and he'd head straight fer the cabinet where he hid his most expensive whiskey.

But I still looked up to him. He was a hero in my eyes. He worked with dangerous men—the Cosa Nostra. My Ma, an Italian chef from Sicily introduced Da to the organisation, and I was thrown into the same dark world.

I loved it.

I reveled in it.

And I became the rebel everyone called me back then.

At sixteen, I'd killed fer the first time. It was life-changing because I was never the same. I had a bloodlust that ran through my veins, and I would satiate it with jobs I did fer the organisation.

It didn't last long. Not when I saw Da gunned down in front of me because he made the Irish Mob angry. They came fer him, and they stole a part of me as well.

I hadn't taken the oath. I wasn't bound to their rules, so I walked away. Ma stayed in Italy, while I returned to Belfast where Da was born and raised. But there wasn't much fer me here. I was too used to the violence of the mafia.

But then I found a new home.

I'm part of a new family.

And even though Ma still calls to talk to me, to make sure I'm alive and well, I haven't seen her since that day she waved to me from the porch of the house I grew up in.

That was three years ago.

Now, I'm a biker. I'm the VP of the Royal Bastards MC, and I'm one of the most dangerous men in the club. And there are a lot of violent feckers in this club house. Monster, the President of the MC, is a man I've known all my life. We grew up in the streets of Belfast. And when he took over the club, it was the mafia who helped with the gun shipments.

It took time for the trust to form. And one night, after we'd done a couple of jobs together, Monster and I were in a pub, fecker knocked me out because we'd been eyein' up the same lassie. He won, and I stepped back. There was respect formin' between us, and that's when I realised we would always be mates.

There is only one thing that weakens me. It's the blonde beauty that's currently lying in the sunshine with her sister, Miren.

Callia has been around the club fer years. And each time I think I'm goin' ta make a move, I remind myself of who she is—the daughter of a man I helped kill.

I want her forgiveness.

But I'm too fecking proud ta ask fer it.

Instead, I plan on breaking her down until she's begging' fer me to claim her.

One day she will, and when that day comes, there will be no escapin' the rabid animal roarin' inside me.

<u>Rebel is available on Amazon</u>

Have you met Monster? If not, dive into the first
book in this romantic suspense series now!
https://geni.us/Xkvu

Or dive into Tye's story, and learn more about the IT
expert of the club…
https://geni.us/lcvHKWq

Catch up on Lucky Clover today
https://geni.us/JOhwx

Spotify

ALSO BY DANI RENÉ

Head to my website here for a full list of my
incredible titles
www.danirene.com

ABOUT THE AUTHOR

Dani is a *USA Today* Bestselling Author of seductive and deviant romance.

Her books range from the dark to emotional, but every hero is alpha, and each heroine is strong-willed, bringing the men down to their knees.

She now lives in the UK, after moving from Cape Town, exploring cemeteries and old buildings while plotting her next book.

When she's not writing, she can be found binge-watching the latest TV series, or working on graphic design. She has a healthy addiction to reading, tattoos, coffee, and ice cream.

www.danirene.com | info@danirene.com
Find me at @danireneauthor on
Facebook | Instagram | Pinterest | TikTok | Spotify